The New Tenant

Allison G. Smith

The New Tenant
Copyright © 2023 by Allison G. Smith

This is a work of fiction. Any characters, businesses, places, events,
and incidents are either the products of the author's imagination
or used in a fictitious manner. Any resemblance to actual persons,
living or dead, or actual events is purely coincidental.

Printed in the United States of America

Hardcover ISBN: 978-1-958714-38-6
Paperback ISBN: 978-1-958714-39-3
Ebook ISBN: 978-1-958714-40-9
Library of Congress Control Number: 2023935608

Muse Literary
3319 N. Cicero Avenue
Chicago IL 60641-9998

For mom and dad.

Thank you for always encouraging me to be me.

ACKNOWLEDGEMENTS

I wish to thank:
Lisa, for your belief and support through this process of reinvention.

Kourtney, for making the introduction that changed everything.

Patti at Muse Literary, for an amazing conversation, for giving me the opportunity, and for the encouragement to "trust the process."

The editorial team, for their enduring patience and guidance.

The friends with whom I shared this journey, for their enthusiasm and optimism.

CHAPTER 1

She grimaces as the hot, thick air strikes her face. Is there anything she can do to stop her hair from frizzing in this humidity? Well, when you come right down to it, does it matter? Her hair had been a source of pride in the days when it was raven black. Who's going to give it a second glance now that it's streaked with silver? And if anyone did, would she want them to?

She smooths her linen skirt and tugs at the sleeves of the jacket. Like her, that suit shows the style of twenty years ago. Tailored to her slim frame, it feels confining and stiff in the damp heat. Her white silk blouse clings to her like a wet tissue. She'd applied her makeup with such care that morning, and now the tiny bead of sweat running down the side of her face threatens to make it run. Frowning, she brushes a stray lock of frizzy hair back from her face and tucks it behind her ear and into the tight bun at the base of her neck.

The heavy, dark wood door closes behind her. The sun is blinding and everything seems washed out. Where, oh where did she leave her sunglasses? Apart from a car moving slowly down the street, nothing stirs. Even the birds are too hot to sing. Her heels clack on the wooden boards of the front porch. A worn front porch, seriously in need of a lick of paint. And what can be done about the slope of the steps? She cares about the state of this house because, although for so many years she lived elsewhere, this is where much of her childhood was spent. The time since then has sometimes been glorious and sometimes has cast her into despair, but all her memories of Beauregard are happy. The railing is sticky under her hand, but there's no way she's going down this incline without care. All she needs at this stage of her life is a broken ankle.

And then out of nowhere the silence is broken by the arrival of a cab. Why would a taxi stop in front of this house?

She's always believed in the value of first impressions. So what are they in this case? He's a little disheveled. The eyes are the key, she knows that, but his Ray-Bans mean she can't see his. Tall, broad shouldered, a solid chest that suggests he could have played football once—but a while ago; this man's young days are well in the past. And who is she to talk? He's probably older than her—but not by much. When she was a girl, her mother used to tell her that harmony in a marriage was most likely when the husband was seven years older than his wife— and the moment she has that thought, she kicks it into the long grass. Husband? Wife? The days when those words might have meant something to her are gone. And that's ignoring the fact that this man hasn't shaved for a while, and creases suggest he might have slept in those clothes.

The trunk pops open and the driver pulls out two suitcases. When he offers to take them into the house, the man shoos him away with a smile. She then realizes, since this taxi drove up, she's stood here observing the newcomer instead of getting on with her day. She's about to move on when he straightens himself up, takes off his glasses, and smiles at her, and she's back in elementary school looking at boyish enthusiasm in all its innocent, infectious glory. And those suitcases—leather, not new but well cared for, probably imported. The man has taste, whatever his other attributes.

"Good morning," he says. "Isn't this a beautiful day?"

"Good morning." She keeps her voice low and starts to walk, but the far-off memories of school return when he speaks like a young boy on his first day in a new class. Life was so different then. So full of promise. Avenues had not been closed off. Doors stood open instead of being firmly shut.

"I'm new here. My name is Jack." He's looking at her as though he expects a response. And politeness demands that he get one.

"Angela." And that's enough of that. It's been a while since any man she didn't know has tried to engage her in conversation. She'd like it to be a while longer, thank you. "Excuse me." And she pushes past him.

"Angela," he says. "Like an angel."

The bus stop. That's all she can think about. She must get to the bus stop and away from this unwelcome irruption into her life. And she does, but when she gets there she half turns, just for a moment, and sees out of the corner of her eye that he is still watching her. Then he turns himself and walks toward the front porch. A new tenant. Obviously. Don't let him be the nuisance he looks as though he could be. Blank him, if necessary. Her mother taught her never to be rude, but sometimes you have to accept that what your mother said does not apply in every situation.

The bus is here. It's easier to avoid engaging with anyone if you sit at the back, so that's what she does, even though the only other passengers are an elderly couple she has seen at the library from time to time. It's hot on the bus and she's ready to fall asleep. Even so, she finds that her mind lingers on the new tenant. She'd rather it didn't, but it does. And she wonders how to reconcile that rumpled look with the leather luggage and the fine, Italian-made shoes that she hadn't at the time even realized she'd noticed.

*   *   *

Jack rolls his cases up the cracked walk toward the house. You only have to look at it to know that it had been something in its day. A distant day, admittedly—Victorian, he would say. That faded, lifeless gray was once the blue of a robin's egg, the dull yellow trim a vivid white. Or perhaps he imagines it—he does that sometimes, and so what? Once upon a time, teachers had told him his imagination would be his fortune. The house is large and sprawling but sheltered, almost embraced, by the maple and oak trees that were probably planted about the time the house was built. Someone keeps the lawn tidy and trimmed, though the grass is brown, which doesn't surprise him when he considers the long, hot summer they are living through. Rain would soon restore it. And rain would bring life back to the parched-looking laurel and rhododendron bushes.

He drags his cases up the steps to the wraparound porch and notices the faded sign over the front door. "Beauregard – Rooms for Let." The hinges creak as he pushes open the door—there'd be no secret, unannounced arrivals here. The room he stands in tells him this was once home to a family with money, and not the rooming house it is now. The crystal chandelier hanging from the high ceiling and the grandfather's clock look as though they've been here as long as the maples and oaks outside.

French doors to his left lead to what looks like a small library. On the other side, a sitting room with a marble fireplace at one end and heavy drapes drawn to keep the sun from further discoloring the already faded Oriental rug. A clicking sound comes from the ancient ceiling fan that is doing nothing to cool the air. The worn armchairs and ottomans might give others a feeling of decay but what Jack experiences is a little different. This is a room in which you could be comfortable.

He rings the ornate bell on the wooden counter at the end of the entry and a deep, robust voice replies, "Can I help you?" Through the doorway from a small dark room behind the counter comes a tall man who is older than Jack but not as old as the house, with a shock of white hair and his reading glasses perched on the tip of his nose. He wears a plaid shirt, faded but clean dungarees, and a tattered blue cardigan.

Jack treats him to a smile. Why not? Jack smiles at almost everyone. "I've come to check in."

"Certainly, sir. Your name?"

"Jack Ford."

"Welcome, Mr. Ford. I'm Bob Russell. I have your room key ready for you."

"Thank you, Mr. Russell. Does your fine establishment have Wi-Fi?"

"You can call me Bob, this establishment isn't so fine, and no. No wi-whatever. There's a coffee shop a couple of blocks away. They have it there."

That's a relief. If there's no access, he can't work.

Bob opens a ledger that looks as old as Jack, and gives him a pen to sign in. "You're on the second floor. I reserve the first for my more elderly residents. Now, Mr. Ford, let me show you to your room."

"Jack . . . please, call me Jack."

Jack picks up his cases and they start up the elaborately carved wooden staircase. As they climb the stairs, Jack says, "Do you actually have many residents right now? There doesn't seem to be anyone around."

"Oh, we're quite full. You'll see the others this evening—right now, they're out and about. There's a library, a park . . . Movies, of course. And there's a senior center a few blocks from here. Apart from the park, they all have air conditioning so right now they are all cooler than this place. First seating for dinner is at five in the afternoon and there'll be plenty of people around by then. If there's anything you need, let me know. If we can provide it, I'll tell you, and if we can't, I'll tell you that, too." Bob stops at the top of the stairs and unlocks a heavy wooden paneled door to a room directly across from the stair landing, swings it open, and hands Jack the keys. "This key is for your room, this is for the front door." Bob starts back down the staircase adding, "See you for dinner."

Jack looks around the modest room, opens his bags, takes out his laptop, notebooks, and papers, and spreads them on his table. It doesn't begin to compare with the five-star hotel rooms he's found himself in around the world but it's clean, it's convenient, and he likes the owner. It will do . . . For now, at least. He came here on a mission, and when that is complete, he'll move out. Until then, this will do just fine. He settles into the easy chair and before he knows it he is asleep.

CHAPTER 2

Angela, too, would like to sleep, but she has no time for frivolities like that. It's four in the afternoon and she's been at the city library all day. Not because it's cool inside, and not because she loves reading, though she does. She comes here to read, yes, but to read as part of her research and the research has one aim. To find a job.

She was a highflyer once. The decision she made to leave her job as marketing director seemed right at the time. Would she make it again? Perhaps. She'd loved the widower she made it for. That isn't in doubt. And she'd loved her life as his second wife—fundraising, charity events, parties, managing the huge Blythewood estate, appearing in the society pages. But he's gone, dead before his time, and almost all his huge wealth went to his children. She was left just enough for room and board at Beauregard, and she wouldn't have had that if her late husband's attorney had not intervened.

People probably thought her stepchildren would help. One of them thought they should. But the other said, "She's not our mother. I know you treat her as though she was, but she isn't. She's an employee who Dad found it convenient to marry when our real mother died. If she'd been anything more, Dad would have written his will differently. It is not for us to decide

he should not have what he wanted, just because he's dead."
Angela knows about those discussions. She holds no grudges.
She had loved her late husband and she thinks he loved her,
but if he had wanted something different, he would have
changed his will to say so. But it did mean she needed a job.
And marketing has changed since her day. It's all digital now.
Online. The few interviews she's had, people talked to her about
search engine optimization, personalization, autoresponders,
and when she looked blank she saw rejection in their faces
long before the words were spoken.

She could accept her new life, become one of the boardinghouse's
old biddies, spend her days in the park in summer and the
library in winter. She has, just, enough money for that. But that
isn't what she was brought up to. She wants to be productive.
She wants to know she has people's esteem as once she had
it. She knows that after twenty years out of the business she's
never going to command the sort of money she once did. But
that doesn't matter. All she needs is to know that she matters
again. Matters as a business professional. And to earn enough
to have a place of her own. Is that so much to ask? Yes, it
sometimes seems that it is.

She has rung the people she used to work with and they
were so encouraging—but nothing happened. Once, she had
been on the inside looking out; now she knows it's a much
harder life on the outside looking in. She's taken courses, and
she comes here to read the textbooks, and she searches the
magazines and newspapers for job advertisements.

It's only when she feels hungry that she realizes it's four
o'clock. She's had nothing to eat since toast and tea at breakfast.
She'd better hurry for the bus, or she'll miss the early seating for
dinner. But now there's one more thing to deal with because,

as she picks up her bag, the sole of her right foot tells her all is not well. She takes off the shoe. There's a hole in the sole. She limps her way to the door but one of the library workers notices. "Is everything all right?" She shows him the shoe and he takes from his cart a roll of duct tape and cuts some pieces to put across the hole. "That will get you home, at any rate."

Grateful, she boards the bus and, once again, sits toward the back. She's had an amazing life—anyone would say that. This time she's going through now is nothing but a bump in the road. She knows that. But, for all her efforts to be positive, tears are pricking at her eyes and it takes an effort of will to stop them from flowing. She will not feel sorry for herself. She will NOT.

Back at Beauregard, she goes straight to the dining room. Originally an immense back porch, Bob's aunt converted it when she started taking boarders. Each room has its own table assigned to it, and Angela's is in a prime position by a window. She can watch birds from here, and see the squirrels scampering around in the grass and gliding up trees.

The house waitress, Wendy, sees Angela through the kitchen door window, bursts through the door, and scurries over to her table with a dinner roll, a pat of butter, and two lemon wedges on a plate. "Good evening, Miss Angela. Cook has a lovely piece of salmon for you. Shall I tell her you're ready for it?"

"Please do, Wendy. I'd like it on a salad, if that's possible." Wendy's friendly presence and the feeling of being where she is welcome send the sadness of the bus journey packing, at least for now. While she waits for the salmon, she pours ice water into a cut glass goblet on the white linen tablecloth and squeezes lemon juice into it. She gazes into the garden; the dining room is filling up and Angela is in no frame of mind for conversation.

A bowl arrives containing fresh greens, cherry tomatoes, chopped cucumber, and sunflower seeds tossed in a light vinaigrette with a perfectly grilled piece of salmon on top. There's just the lightest touch of dill on the salmon and Angela finds the whole assembly delicious, but when Wendy offers dessert she shakes her head. "Nothing for me, Wendy. But please thank Cook for me—the salmon was wonderful."

Leaving the dining room, she meets Jack coming in. His expression says he's going to speak to her, and she cannot suppress a shudder. All she wants is her own space. Jack says, "We meet again! Have you eaten?"

"I have," she says, easing her way past him. But he doesn't seem to want to let her go.

"A pity," he says. "Here in a new place, I'd love some company."

At that point, Wendy comes out of the kitchen and greets him. "Hello, Mr. Ford—I'm Wendy. Let me show you to your table."

"Thank you, Wendy," he says. "I'll be right with you." To Angela, he says, "Perhaps we might sit out in the yard afterwards? You can tell me all about your day."

She has no intention of talking to anyone about her day, and especially not to someone so brash and presumptuous. It's time to put him in his place. "No, thank you," she says. "Good evening." And she heads for the stairs.

Wendy takes Jack to his table, leans forward, and speaks softly enough that no one else can hear. "Miss Angela pretty much keeps to herself, Mr. Ford. She's had quite a time of it, and yet she's still so generous. We all love her."

"Thanks for the advice, Wendy. What do you mean by 'quite a time of it'?"

"Well, that's her story for her to tell. I'm sure she will if she wants to. She can be quite wary around new people. Here's our menu card. What can I get for you?"

The choices are rather limited, but the beef stroganoff with green beans turns out to be better than he might have expected in a boardinghouse. And then Wendy persuades him to take some chocolate mousse for dessert. He takes in the joyful, boho way she dresses and realizes in the nick of time that commenting on a skirt that would not look out of place on a Hungarian gypsy is not guaranteed to be well received. Instead, he says, "Those are striking earrings."

The way she touches one of her marcasite and amethyst drops suggests she takes pride in them. "Miss Angela gave me these last Christmas. From her own private collection."

A lifetime's practice in watching other people tells Jack that most of the residents here are friendly, welcoming, but perhaps a little out of place. The feeling he gets is that many of these regular tenants are misfits of one sort or another—people who have lived interesting lives and somehow ended up here. He likes the idea because misfits can be much more interesting than "normal" people—whatever normal people may be. He came here for a specific purpose and when the purpose is fulfilled he'll leave, but until then interesting people are better to be around than the boring kind. He wasn't sure about Beauregard when he booked it. If this town had had somewhere more like his usual five-star stays, he wouldn't be here. He feels just the hint of satisfaction that the luxury option had not been available.

CHAPTER 3

Jack's first night in his new home had been more comfortable than anyone without his history of regularly turning up in upscale hotels around the world might have expected. Now he's at the coffee shop with his laptop and folio, and he's wondering what to make of it. It's clean, which is good, but what else would you say about it? Eccentric? Slightly crazed? Maybe it's just Middle America. Maybe he's been a city boy too long. The place has a touch of Norman Rockwell about it. When he was younger, he'd have laughed at Rockwell—sentimental nonsense—but the older he gets, the more drawn he is to that vision of America. There's a long wood counter and a bunch of pastry stands—each with a cover, and each empty at this point in the morning. There are stools at the counter, and scattered around the old wooden floor are a number of equally old wood tables and chairs. None of the tables and none of the chairs match each other; some are painted, some aren't, and some are a mixture of the two. The products of several trips to a flea market? He wonders what people who work in a place like this must be like. And he finds out, because when he opened the door a bell had rung and a young woman behind the counter has turned to check out her visitor. "What can I get you?"

She may be pretty behind the dark circles under her eyes, but what strikes him most is the piercing gaze from hazel eyes staring at him, summing him up, from a pale, unmade-up face. When he doesn't immediately answer her question she says, "I'm not here for people to gawk at. Do you want something, or don't you? I have plenty of other things I can be doing."

Her directness startles him. "Sorry," he says. "Still a bit early. Sure, I'll have a café au lait."

"Coffee with milk. Okay." She pours coffee from a glass pot into a brown mug. "Medium roast is all that's ready this early. Milk and everything else is over there."

"Medium roast is fine. Thank you."

But when he takes a bill from his wallet she says, "Fifty dollars? You're the first customer today. I won't be able to break anything that big for at least an hour."

Jack goes through his wallet and finds a ten-dollar bill. "Keep the change. I believe you have Internet here?"

She ignores his suggestion about the change and puts a five and some small coins on the counter. "Wi-Fi credentials are on the sign over there. Anything else?"

He picks up the five, and leaves the coins. He feels like he's been given a lesson in the etiquette expected in this particular coffee shop. "That's it for now, thank you." He gives his best and most engaging smile. There is no response. She doesn't snarl at him, doesn't look hostile, but nor does she smile back. He goes to a table by the window in the furthest corner and sits with his back to the wall, facing the shop and the windows where he can see anyone who comes in. "Can't be too careful," he says. "You never know when Jesse James might show up." But it's a wasted effort. She's gone back to preparing for the day and, if she even heard him, she isn't going to let it show.

He fires up his laptop, opens a notebook, and starts working through formulas and sketches. He makes entries on a spreadsheet and then pulls up a picture of a young girl which he gazes at for a few moments. Customers have begun to come in, all apparently regulars because they seem to know the woman behind the counter. He gathers that her name is Kara. She's constantly on the move, pouring drinks, serving baked goods, clearing tables, refilling sugar dispensers, topping off coffee cups. When she refills his, he tries to engage her in conversation but all he gets is a half smile. He realizes it's nothing personal—she isn't particularly friendly or chatty with other customers, either.

As the morning rush subsides, Jack approaches a table Kara is scrubbing. "Is it all right if I hang out for a while? The place I'm staying doesn't have Internet and . . ."

"You must be at the boardinghouse down the street. It's no problem to me. Just buy something from time to time and don't bother the customers and the owner won't care if you sit there all day."

"Good. You'll be seeing a lot of me, then."

"Oh, goodie."

Is she being sarcastic? He doesn't know her well enough to say. Whatever, she's letting him know where the boundaries are. He says, "I'm Jack, by the way," and is not at all surprised when she doesn't reply. He works on, but not all his mind is focused on what's on the screen in front of him. He is also thinking about Angela. She, too, had set clear boundaries; in her case, he'd like to put them to the test. Why we should be happy to be ignored by some people but long to be welcomed into the lives of others he has no idea. But that's how it is. And it's a long time since he wanted to make a friend of anyone as much as he wants to make one of Angela.

*   *   *

That evening, Angela is once again at her table by the window early. She has a book open in front of her, but she's aware that Jack is strolling toward her with an air of nonchalance that she thinks is assumed. He says, "Good evening."

He's given it his best smile, but she isn't going to be warmed by a smile. She looks up, says, "Good evening," and goes back to her book.

He should have gone to his own table after that, but he still stands there. He says, "How was your day?" And then, as if that was not intrusive enough, "Would you like company at dinner?"

When she was on the board, she was famed for her ability to put people in their place if they made it necessary. She hasn't lost it. She knows the look she gives him is cold, because cold is what she means it to be. She says, "Thank you, but I prefer to eat alone." And, once again, she returns her attention to her book.

Then Wendy is there and Angela is treated to a little show that gives her an insight into aspects of this importunate man's life when Wendy says, "Mr. Ford, housekeeping asked me to let you know they can't clean your room with all the papers strewn about. They're afraid of disturbing something important."

Is he irritated by this interruption? Angela thinks he is. He was not going to give up on his attempt to insert himself into her existence. And now he has to. She hears him say, "Oh, well, that's just the way I work. Tell them not to bother with my room for now." Angela keeps her head down because, difficult as it is to understand, he is looking at her as though he intends to speak again. Where on earth was he brought up? Has he no sense of when someone doesn't want to hear from him? Where are his social antennae?

But Wendy, who knows Angela's ways very well, comes to her rescue. "I understand, Mr. Ford, but please let me know when would be a convenient time and I'll pass the information on to them. And now, if you'd like to take a seat at your table, I'll take your order for dinner."

She can sense his annoyance that Wendy has interrupted his attempts to break into her solitude. For herself, she is grateful. But now she sees the drawback that she didn't understand the previous evening because she had left the dining room just as he arrived. She'd have much preferred the table they have given him to be on the other side of the room, but it isn't. It's near hers. She bends more closely to her book, intent on sending him the clearest possible signal that she does not want his conversation.

Cook has excelled herself tonight. The roast chicken falls off the bone and almost melts in the mouth. The roast potatoes and vegetables are full of flavor. She feels an irrational pride that this man who attempted to force his company on her is seeing that this nondescript boardinghouse offers fare rivalling acclaimed restaurants in major metropolitan cities. And through it all, she is aware of his skill in engaging in small talk not just with Wendy but with others in the dining room. He seems to know something about everything. He entertains everyone he converses with. She watches, without seeming to. His gregariousness seems to be genuine. Perhaps all he wants is to be friendly with everyone. Perhaps she may have been too short with him. Perhaps a conversation might after all be a pleasure. But it would have to be on her terms and not on his. She returns to her book. This time, she decides to stay in the dining room long enough to eat dessert. But, though still talking easily to others, he does not look at or speak to her again.

CHAPTER 4

To her great surprise, Angela had spent the rest of her evening concerned that she had perhaps been too quick to dismiss the friendship offered by Jack Ford. It wasn't a huge concern—not something she was likely to lose sleep over—but it did seem possible that she might have been just a little hasty. And she seemed to have done a good job of repelling him, because he had not looked up even when she left the dining room, despite her having walked closer to his table than was strictly necessary. Oh, well, if she'd closed that door without enough thought it was done and there was no point beating herself up over it.

In fact, she was worrying about nothing. Jack Ford is an engineer. He's spent the whole of his working life meeting challenges and overcoming them. Challenges are what he likes. Angela has become a challenge. And there's no hurry—they live in the same house. He won't be going anywhere for a while and she looks like a fixture. A challenge takes the time it takes. His father had inherited from *his* father an old-style gramophone and a bunch of 78 rpm records. As a boy, those records had been the background to so much of his life, not listened to but absorbed in any case. He remembers one about letting the earth take a couple of whirls and finding that the girl who had rejected you rejects you no longer. So that's what he plans to do. Let the earth take a couple of whirls, and see what happens. And he doesn't intend to forget an important lesson he learned years ago. People want most what they can't have. If you seem keen to have their friendship, they may think themselves above you. If you ignore them, they will often feel the need to attract your attention. In the meantime, he has an appetite for breakfast and, who knows? Angela may be present when he eats it. Afterward, he'll head for the coffee shop and the Wi-Fi.

He showers and pulls on a casual shirt and slacks. If Angela does happen to be at breakfast at the same time as him, it can't hurt to make a good impression. Even if he takes care to ignore her.

Anyone watching him skip down the stairs would be forgiven for thinking they were seeing a much younger man. Some of the other tenants are already in the dining room. Their breakfasts are a little on the sparse side. Toast. Tea or coffee. In some cases, a boiled egg. What Angela eats he will not find out this time, because she isn't here. As he takes his seat, Wendy appears from the kitchen. "Shall I have Cook make you a nice, healthy breakfast?"

"I'm sure whatever the pair of you come up with will be fine with me."

She smiles and disappears into the kitchen. When she comes back nearly ten minutes later, she places before him a huge omelet with mushrooms and Swiss cheese, home fries, seared tomato slices, and whole grain toast. Freshly squeezed orange juice is a nice surprise and she pours him a cup of coffee from a fresh pot. "Cook doesn't often have the chance to make a proper breakfast." She leans a little closer and lowers her voice. "She'd never admit it, but I think she's pleased to have someone here who enjoys a big meal. Some of our older residents . . . I love them all, but many of them have very small appetites."

As he prepares to leave, he looks around in what he thinks is a surreptitious way, but Wendy has come to clear his plates and she isn't fooled. Once again speaking quietly, she says, "She generally doesn't have much of a breakfast during the week."

He is astonished to find himself blushing—something he hasn't done for many years. "Oh, dear. Was it that obvious?"

Wendy smiles. "She's already left. She's never late for dinner, though. Ah . . . But you won't see her tonight. I happen to know she's having dinner with her stepson."

*   *   *

When he gets to the coffee shop, he sits at the same table and opens his laptop. Kara is loading fresh baked goods into a case on the front counter. She yells across the empty room. "Coffee?"

Jack looks up. It has to be him she's talking to—there's no one else here. "Oh, yes, please," he shouts back. His smiles had got him nowhere yesterday, but he tries another one now.

Kara brings a mug and a pot of steaming coffee. "Just be sure to keep that mug filled so customers don't think I'm letting you squat here."

"I need the Wi-Fi, so whatever it takes to stay, I'll . . ." But he stops talking because she has walked away.

He works steadily until the middle of the afternoon at which point, full of coffee, he closes his laptop and leaves to wander the streets. It's time he took inventory of the place he's come to live. This must once have been an area of grand houses, but now most of the remaining old places are in disrepair and the rest have been replaced by more modern housing. When he gets back to Beauregard, it's still too early for dinner and so he goes up to his room to work through some ideas in his notebook. And then it's five o'clock and he's back in the dining room wondering what's on tonight's menu.

When his dinner arrives, it's impossible not to see that he has at least twice as many potatoes and asparagus spears as most of the guests and a piece of fish double the size of what they are eating. He also notes that he has two bread rolls, not one, and two pats of butter. And it's all delicious.

Other diners smile and nod to him and one or two who are close enough speak. He's been accepted in his new home—but then, he's used to that. He's always had this ability to make friends. But there's still one friend he would particularly like to make.

So, she has a stepson, has she? There's a story there. And Jack wants to know what it is. A stepson means she was married once. Where is the husband now? Is he dead? And if she was married, the impression she gives of wanting nothing to do with men can't be the whole story. There's no hurry. Jack will find out. In the end, he always does.

CHAPTER 5

There's more than a century between the faded magnificence of Beauregard and this modern, high-rise apartment block in which Angela finds herself this evening. Is there any trace of her in this tall young man with tousled blond hair in his white shirt and jeans? In his manner, perhaps, but not in his appearance because, though she raised him from a child, Jon carries another mother's genes. "Hello, my love," she says. "How are you? And what is that amazing smell?"

"I made something special, just for us."

"Just for us? Heather isn't here?"

"Girls' night out. Which is fine with me—I get you all to myself."

The living room is huge, its style minimalist, with everything in calming shades of gray and sky blue. There is a fireplace, but you couldn't burn logs in it; the only fuel it accepts is gas. Hanging above it, a large abstract painting in a stainless frame. Black and white fine art photography arranged as if in a gallery. One wall is nothing but windows; one of the things Angela loves about coming here is the view over the city, even more attractive now when lights are beginning to twinkle as the day fades. Another is getting time with her favorite stepchild. "You always know exactly what I need to hear to feel good."

"You're my mother. I've had a lot of practice."

"You should never forget ..."

"I don't. But she died when I was still a baby. I have no memory of her. You're the only mom I've ever known, and no one could have had a better one. My brother doesn't get it, but that's his problem."

They are moving toward dangerous ground. Time to change the subject. "How are the wedding plans going?"

"Slowly." He looks up from the salad he is tossing. "Heather hasn't liked any of the wedding planners we've met with, and she thinks everything will just happen as if by magic. It's becoming a little frustrating." He opens a bottle of wine, pours a glass for Angela and one for himself, and goes back to the salad. But he's looking sideways at her. "Ange ..."

She knows that long drawn out sound of old. It has always meant he is plotting something. "What are you cooking up now? I mean, apart from dinner?"

"How many events did you plan for Dad?"

She freezes. She senses what is coming and, although she is flattered, she is not best friends with Heather. Heather is Jon's choice and Angela wouldn't say a word against her, but if she didn't get along with the wedding planners offered to her so far, it's not easy to imagine that she would warm to anything suggested by Angela.

Jon goes on, "All those charity and company events. And every single one done with class and style." He slaps his forehead. "Why didn't I think of it before? It's obvious. You should plan our wedding."

"Jon, I'm flattered. But that's a decision for the bride to make and not the groom and I don't believe Heather would welcome it. If nothing else, she'll think any suggestions I might make will be outdated. Passé." She smiles to take the sting out of her words. "As I am myself."

"Nonsense. I'll speak to her tomorrow. Perhaps I'll wait till the afternoon, she's more likely to be coherent again then."

"You can do that as long as you make it clear to her that this is your suggestion and not mine and that all I offered in reply was objections and drawbacks. Because I don't think she'll like the idea. And now let's forget about it and just enjoy our evening."

He pulls a tray of scallops out of the broiler and plates several on a bed of couscous with a butter lettuce salad on the side. That's another reason she loves coming here—he knows exactly the kind of food she likes. The scallops are seasoned perfectly, the wine is an excellent match, and the meal goes with a swing.

When it's over and everything has been cleared away, he shows her photographs he's taken for marketing materials and a possible book for the international aid group he works for. She loves that he's found something he enjoys that matches his talents. She'd had to intervene several times to head off his father's discontent that Jon, unlike his older brother, was not cut out for the family business. If she hadn't, his father might not have left him the generous stipend that lets him lead a comfortable life following the path he has chosen for himself. She's proud of the way he has developed into a caring, loving, intelligent young man.

Just for this one night, she is able to revel in the kind of life she had once lived. And then it's growing late, and she turns down his offer to drive her home. "It's too late, and you've had too many glasses of wine. I'll take the bus."

"Ange . . . It's late. At least let me call you a cab."

"Jon, I have no money for taxis."

"I'll pay. Of course. We shouldn't be having this conversation anyway—there's a corner bedroom in this apartment with its own bathroom. You could move in there and then you wouldn't have to worry about how you got home in the evening."

She takes a deep breath. They've had this conversation before and she had hoped that his engagement to Heather had finally put it to bed. "You know I can't do that. Heather isn't going to want to know your stepmother is lurking about the place. And I'm comfortable in Beauregard. It has happy memories for me. It's fine. I'm fine."

"I won't give up. I want to be here for you. You've always been there for me."

"And that's very sweet. But you ARE there for me and you've been so generous."

"Not generous enough. You got a raw deal and my brother's behavior has been disgraceful."

"Jon . . . It's fine. I get it."

"If Dad had known he was going to die so suddenly, he'd have changed his will instead of always putting it off because he was too busy with other things."

"Let's not end the evening this way." She tousles his hair with her hand. "You've been a fantastic support and I love you for it. And now I have to go."

He comes down with her in the elevator, hails a car, and puts her in it. He leans into the passenger-side window and hands the driver a hundred-dollar bill. "Take this lady wherever she wants to go. Then take ten percent of the fare for your tip and give the rest of the change to her."

The kindness, the generosity are so like her late husband's virtues, she has to wipe away a tear. She waves to him from the back seat as the car draws away. It's been a good evening.

Jon has reinvented himself, away from family expectations and pressures. And if he can, so can she.

*   *   *

It's much later than she had meant to get home. But for the porch lights and a lamp glowing in the front sitting-room window, the house is dark. She closes the car door carefully behind her to avoid waking residents and takes care on the squeaky front steps for the same reason—but when she turns her key in the front door the loud click makes her pause. She pushes the door open slowly and closes it as quietly as possible. Every time a step creaks on her way to her room, she cringes. She doesn't want to wake anyone and nor does she want people commenting on how late she got home. At the top of the stairs she tiptoes along the worn carpet runners, unlocks and opens a door, and locks it again behind her. Up two more steps to another door on the landing leading to a bathroom and a few more steps winding up to the right to a large room in the turret. This is her private space, the place where she feels most secure. She turns on a lamp just inside the room and realizes that she has been holding her breath.

This turret room was once an attic. When she moved here, Bob and Wendy spent a week clearing everything away and scrubbing and polishing the room. They whitewashed the walls, cleaned the beveled glass windows, and hung pale curtains with lace sheers so that the room would be sunny but not too bright. They refinished and polished the wooden floor to be smooth under her feet. Fluffy, soft pale pink and blue rugs are scattered over the floor. There is a white wrought iron bed at the end of the room covered in lace-trimmed sheets and pillowcases, handsewn quilts, a comforter, and crocheted and lace pillows. This is her respite from the world. On a night table is a crystal lamp, one of the few things she was able to bring from her former life, along with an alarm clock, a radio tuned to the local classical station, and a stack of books. In the curve of the windows is a silver-gray vanity table holding crystal bottles and jars of various sizes and colors, a vase of flowers she fills with whatever offers itself around the garden, and a sterling silver dressing table set engraved with her initials—a present from her late husband. At the other end of the room is a tall dresser and more books. There are no closets, but Bob set up three clothes racks covered in canvas. Around the room are small tables with porcelain figures and pictures in silver frames—and more books. In the corner are an oversized upholstered chair and ottoman striped blue-gray and cream, a table, and a reading lamp.

Since she lost her husband, this room is the center of her life. What comfort she has is here. And she knows how to make the best of it, because the life she led before was so busy she never had time to curl up in a comfortable chair and read. In this room she can feel at home in a house she loved long before she even thought of marriage. As for the future—it will be what it will be. But as for Jon's suggestion that she arrange the wedding—well, she would love it but Heather will hate the idea so she puts it right out of her mind. It will never happen. But she does have seventy dollars she didn't have before, the change the taxi driver gave her from Jon's hundred. She knows it's Jon's generosity—his way of giving her money without it seeming an act of charity. And she's happy to accept it. It will probably pay the price of getting her shoes fixed.

CHAPTER 6

Jack is settling in. Most mornings he goes to the coffee shop to work; some afternoons he strolls around the neighborhood, goes to a local bookstore, or sometimes there will be an outdoor concert in the park. As summer's oppressive heat eases, he sits in the backyard to read his newspaper or scientific journals and review notes on projects he is working on. This little bubble, with its disconnection from the busyness of the outside world, seems to give more time for thought. The slowed-down pace of life agrees with him.

He sees Angela each day, always in a hurry . . . A hurry to get out in the morning, a hurry to get an early seat for dinner, a hurry to run up to her room. Maybe it isn't just him—she could simply be one of nature's introverts.

Something else about the house that interests him is Wendy and her relationship with Bob and the other residents. Bit by bit, in conversations with Bob, with Wendy herself, and with other residents, he pieces her story together. She's an only child, now in her early twenties, and her parents died in a car accident when she was in her teens. She was old enough to take care of herself and finish high school but she needed somewhere safe to live. Bob provided it. She has a small room to herself, good meals, and Bob pays her just enough to study business and hospitality management at the local community college. And that's where what problems there are arise. Wendy's dream is one day to own her own hotel in some exotic beach location. In the meantime, she has ideas about how Beauregard can be improved. And Bob likes things just the way they are.

Wendy and the others have also shared enough bits about Bob for Jack to piece together. Bob has lived in the house almost his entire life. His aunt owned it originally and, when she died, Bob was a young man studying law. Having no children of her own, she left the house to him. He wanted to sell it and finish school, but he just couldn't bring himself to turn out tenants that had relied on his aunt to provide a place—and care—for them. He left college and moved in to take over her business. He hasn't made many improvements in the decades he's been here, but the house is clean and tidy and he insists on keeping an excellent cook. A good meal is the one indulgence he allows himself for giving up his dreams of being an attorney.

They bicker sometimes like father and daughter. But the bond between them, and the affection they have for each other, are obvious.

As time goes by, Jack sees a few new people come and others leave. Wendy plagues Bob until he has the sign repainted so that people can see there are rooms to rent. But it's observing the longtime residents that Jack most enjoys. Wendy loves talking to him and telling him things. He realizes there's nothing personal about that—she is the same with everyone. Bit by bit, he learns their backstories.

Paulina and Herman, for example. They shuffle into the dining room like the elderly couple they are, eat their frugal meals in silence showing impeccable manners, and shuffle out again. Herman is tall with wavy silver hair and a pleasant face that always seems to be ever so slightly smiling. Paulina is at least a foot shorter than him, her shock of white hair impeccably styled and her makeup applied with a light touch. They dress conservatively in dark colors, but Paulina usually has a silk scarf and a glittering brooch or other piece of jewelry saved from their life before they came here. When they sit in the garden or on the front porch, Herman always seems to have his nose in an ancient book and Paulina will be reading something lighter or doing some kind of needlework. They give the impression that the Sunday newspaper is the highlight of their week. Herman devours every word and Paulina spends the morning completing all the puzzles. What Jack learns is that they never had children; as they grew older, their home became too great a burden and they now live off the proceeds of selling it together with Herman's pension. They spend a lot of time at the senior citizen center where it seems Paulina is a bingo enthusiast.

Then there's Henry, a retired salesman who spent his entire career on the road and never married or made a home. When his company told him it was time to retire, he came to Beauregard because he had nowhere else to go. Jack sees him sometimes, helping Bob with yard work and minor repairs and polishing fixtures around the house. You only have to look at him to know that Henry likes to be productive and helpful, always busy and on the move.

Stella and Louise are two sisters who never stop talking to each other. All the years they've spent together and still they have things to talk about. And they earn their keep—they are the ones who keep the rooms on the main floor polished and gleaming. They are very friendly and it gives Jack great pleasure to greet them at dinner each evening and make them giggle.

As the weather cools and autumn colors appear, walking through the neighborhood becomes a pleasure. This area is mostly residential, and quiet. While walking, Jack sees people cleaning up their yards and mowing grass. The clean, cool air is a welcome respite from the heat and humidity of high summer and the lawn in front of the house has lost its parched, burned appearance.

*   *   *

Angela, too, is enjoying the change in the climate. One morning, just as she's finishing breakfast of whole grain toast and tea, Jack arrives. "Good morning," he says. "Are you enjoying this cooler weather as much as I am?"

And Angela astonishes herself when she hears her own voice say, "Yes, thank goodness. This time of year is much more pleasant." There. It's done. She's avoided him for weeks, but the knowledge that, really, she'd quite like to talk to him has steadily grown. His friendliness is not directed only at her—it's genuine, and everyone in the house seems to like him. In refusing to speak, she is hurting only herself. And, really, how can anyone resist that boyish enthusiasm forever? That zest—that willingness to see the positive instead of the negative—has been missing from her life for too long. She experienced it at full blast in her earlier years as a company director and then again when she was married to one of the most energetic people she's ever known. It died when he did. Or so she thought. Does Jack present an opportunity to have it back?

Jack takes a seat at the next table. He says, "Are you doing anything interesting today?"

She makes herself speak, casting aside the caution that has ruled her for so long. "I'm going to the city library."

"Oh. I keep meaning to go but somehow I haven't got round to it yet. Do you go often?"

"Just about every day." She feels her guard going up—that's enough questions for one morning. And it seems Jack understands because he asks nothing else.

Instead, he says, "I find pretty much everything I need for my work online. The Wi-Fi is reliable at the coffee shop down the road . . ." Has he sensed her attention wandering? He's certainly stopped speaking. So she can add sensitivity to the moods and needs of others to his other gifts. She folds her napkin and stands. Should she say she'll see him later? On balance, she thinks not—she's gone quite far enough for one day.

But instead of ignoring him as she usually does she says, "Good morning." And then she leaves the room, collects her things, and sets off for the bus stop.

*   *   *

After she's gone, it takes Jack a few moments to realize that the dining room is silent. He was so busy congratulating himself on finally having made some kind of breakthrough with Angela that he did not notice that the attention of everyone present has been focused on the exchange. And they are all smiling at him! He looks around in astonishment—and then he smiles himself. One by one, the other residents go back to their breakfasts and their conversations, but Jack is left trying to remember when—if ever—he has been part of such a close-knit group. It's as if everyone here has an interest in seeing his friendship with Angela blossom.

When his own breakfast is over, his walk to the coffee shop has just a little more spring in his step than usual. Kara looks even more frazzled than she normally does, so Jack says hello, orders his coffee, and goes to his usual table without saying anything else. From time to time while he's working he glances at her over the top of his laptop. She seems quiet. As if something is worrying her.

And then he sees something else. Is it the way Kara's face just happens to be tilted at the same angle as one he's become accustomed to? He pulls up on his screen the photo of a young girl he's looked at in the past. He looks at it. He looks at Kara. He looks again at the picture on the screen and then again at Kara. He compares them. The nose. The eyes. The hair. Surely, it's impossible? Surely it can't be . . . But it is. It must be. The one he's been looking for. The girl he came to find, one of the reasons he came here. It's her. Kara. He's found her.

But how does he handle this? How does he introduce himself? How does he explain? How does he make things right?

He doesn't want to confront her here where she works and anyone could come in in the middle of what promises to be a fraught conversation. He needs to know where she lives. Perhaps the best plan might be a seemingly accidental meeting between her home and here. He brings up his email, finds an address in his contact list, and taps out a message.

He can't concentrate. Just focusing on what he's trying to read is impossible, all thoughts driven out of his head as he imagines a joyful reunion and the things he can do for her. It's no good trying to battle on here, and so he starts to gather his papers together. As he is about to rise from his seat, his phone pings. He has a text message. It gives him an address. The address is not far away. Not only is it nearby, it's on his route from the boardinghouse to here. How lucky can one man be? What made him zero in on this neighborhood? Of course there's no way of knowing, but he feels so glad. He takes a last look at Kara as he leaves. He thinks about how we can never know the future, but how his hopes have just risen.

*   *   *

When Jack enters the dining room that evening, he realizes he's a little late. Most of the residents are seated. Some are already partway through their meals. Of course, one resident matters more to Jack than any of the others and when he looks at Angela's table he sees she was there before him but hasn't yet been served her meal. He says, "Good evening. What a lovely day. Such a relief to be rid of that oppressive heat." He has no particular expectation of a reply, but no one as enthusiastic as Jack ever completely gives up hope.

And he's right not to, because Angela smiles and gives him more than the abrupt one or two words he's come to expect. "Yes," she says. "It is a relief." And then after the briefest of pauses she says, "So. What do you do with your days?"

He can't believe it. Is this another breakthrough, or is he imagining it? Seize the moment. He says, "I got some work done today. Started a new project. And then I took a walk around the neighborhood. There's an amazing amount to do in this little burg."

"Oh? I hadn't really noticed."

She's avoiding eye contact. Her caution hasn't completely disappeared, then. But he presses on. "Oh, yes. There's a lovely park not far from here. And the town website has a calendar of events. Some of them sound enticing. In a couple of weeks, there's going to be a concert by an all-volunteer symphony orchestra. And just round the corner from the coffee shop is a quaint little bookstore."

"Well, you have been busy. I knew about the orchestra, of course, but I've never been to a concert. It's not something I would do alone."

And at just that point, the conversation is interrupted by Wendy bringing Angela's dinner. He isn't going to complain, because compared to how she has treated him since his arrival, the conversation they've just had was someone else's garrulous gossip. And that last sentence—that she wouldn't go to a concert on her own. Is it even possible there was a hint there? That she might enjoy a concert if someone went with her? Someone . . . Like him? Normally, he would have put that to the test straight away by suggesting he buy tickets for two. He congratulates himself on avoiding the temptation. He knows how he often seems—a bundle of bouncing enthusiastic energy. He also knows, or at least thinks he knows, that Angela is not attracted by that enthusiasm. Might even, in fact, be repelled. That's all right. He will bide his time. But if that really was a signal, he'll be watching for another. And next time, he will respond to it.

Dinner is baked cod with brown rice and steamed spinach. Just right for the time of year and the weather. There's a hint in the rice's nutty flavor that white wine was used in its preparation. The fish is lightly seasoned with herbs and baked to perfection. The spinach has been heated till it wilted, but not overcooked.

And then comes dessert—a mouthwatering apple cobbler with a dollop of fresh whipped cream. Wendy tells them Cook has a deal with a local orchard and the apples were picked from the tree just that morning.

*   *   *

Angela usually makes sure that she has left the table by the time Jack finishes his meal. This evening, she hasn't done that. She isn't sure why and she doesn't want to examine her motives too closely. Jack says, "Since the weather changed I've been sitting out in the backyard after dinner to read my newspaper in the cool evening air. Would you like to join me?"

His tone is casual—but what about his motivation? She can't deny she'd like a little time outside in the open air. She rarely sits in the backyard. Or on the front porch, for that matter. When you come right down to it, she almost never sits in any of the public rooms. Usually, she goes straight to her own room at the top of the house. For comfort? Well, yes, that's certainly part of the reason. But does she go also for security? And if she does, does she want to examine in her heart of hearts exactly what it is she wants security against? Overall, she thinks not. "Oh," she says. "Well . . . I don't think so."

"It's such a beautiful evening. I just want to breathe in the fresh air. And you might enjoy the paper's arts and leisure section?"

And that's the killer, though not in the way that he may have intended. If he only knew how often she'd been featured in that section of the newspaper. For fundraising events, for her beautiful estate home, for her marriage to a powerful man.

No. She can't face it. "No, I don't think so. But thank you." And she's on her feet and leaving the dining room in as much hurry as she usually does.

*   *   *

What has he said? Rising from the table, he plays the conversation in his head looking for the exact moment when he lost her. At the desk, he sees Beauregard's owner. "Bob. Good evening. Any mail for me?"

From under his desk, Bob pulls out scientific magazines and a couple of newspapers. "You're a man who likes to stay informed."

"Oh, yes. Need to stay on top of business while I'm here."

"Business?"

"I mean things. You know. Things."

"Jack. Do you mind if I say something personal?"

"I don't when other people do it." He laughs. "And, believe me, people have said some very personal things to me over the years. So go ahead."

"It's about Angela."

"Oh. Yes?" Is he about to be warned off?

"You're drawn to her. Aren't you?"

"Well . . . Yes. She's . . ."

"And I don't blame you. We are all very fond of Angela here. But she's had a rough old time of it. Lost her husband and had nowhere to go but here."

"Wow—that's rough. But why this place? Surely she had a home?"

"She lost it when her husband died. And she had a connection with Beauregard, because my aunt took care of her when she was a child, so this is a comfortable, familiar place for her."

"Oh, I see. You know her well, then?"

"Not really. Or not until she came to live here, at any rate. By the time I took over this house from my aunt, Angela was in school. Her days running around these halls were behind her."

"Right. I see. So this is a safe place for her."

"It seems so. And she's got a place here as long as she wants it. Adds a little class to Beauregard, if you ask me."

"You are so right." He picks up his journals and newspapers, cuts back through the dining room to the backyard, and heads to a little spot he likes to relax and do some reading in.

*   *   *

From a window in the upstairs hallway, Angela peeks round the curtain and watches Jack settle himself in a chair under one of the willow trees. She goes on to her room and tries to be calm, but her mind is a jumble. *What's wrong with me? The past is the past; it's over and done with. I have to stop feeling sorry for myself. And I have to stop being afraid. He's just trying to be friendly. What harm can come from that?*

She lets herself into her room, closes the door behind her, sits on her bed, and curls up with a soft coverlet and a book. Usually, she can distract herself from anything this way. This evening, it isn't proving so easy.

At last she falls asleep, dreaming of her former home and her old life.

CHAPTER 7

The days pass, as days do. Angela makes her daily trips to the library, attends any free workshops going, and eats dinner listening to Jack rambling about world events, scientific breakthroughs, and the surprising first edition he found at the local bookstore. Jack goes to the coffee shop, works on projects, and—though Angela can know nothing about this—rehearses in his head possible ways to approach Kara that would end in a joyful reconciliation. He certainly keeps himself busy, she can see that. And she's beginning to find his banter not only reliable but somehow comforting. She almost looks forward to dinner, though she avoids that knowledge. Some of his dinner conversation seems familiar; her late husband had often shared exciting engineering advances and technological breakthroughs at the dinner table. Not that she would in any way compare Jack and the man she'd been married to. Jack could never be a replacement. But perhaps he might possibly be company?

One Friday evening, dinner eaten, Jack bids Angela good evening and follows her from the dining room. She is making for the staircase and he for the front desk. Taking a deep breath, she turns to face him. "Will you be sitting out in the garden this evening?"

"I most certainly will!"

Her will almost fails her. With an effort not visible on the outside but almost tearing her apart on the inside she says, "Would you like some company?"

"I should love it."

Jack gathers his paper and some technical journals Bob has laid out for him. Then he and Angela walk through the now empty dining room, spotless with scrubbed floor and chairs and tabletops wiped down. Every chair is pushed neatly under its table and the tables are arranged perfectly corner to corner with every other table in a row down the middle of the room, while the tables at the sides of the room are perfectly spaced to allow access to chairs by the wall or the window. The curtains are drawn and the room is uncharacteristically quiet, as if resting for tomorrow's bustle. They pass through the makeshift greenhouse into the backyard. The grass is trimmed and edged and recovering well from the summer heat. Square stepping stones lead to a small patio in various shades of slate, some pieces cracked or broken. Behind the small patio, tall bushes surround and shelter the entire backyard. A decades-old willow drapes its tendrils over the patio providing shade and making a cozy and secluded space.

Jack has placed a lawn chair and small table on the patio and this is where he likes to spend the early evenings reading. He grabs another chair from those scattered around the yard and places it on the other side of the table. He pulls out his handkerchief, brushes off both chairs, repositions the cushions, and gestures that Angela should use the first chair which she can see is the more sturdy and reliable of the two. "Well," he says. "It's nice to have company for a change."

"Does no one else sit back here?"

"Just me. I think the ground may be too uneven for the more elderly residents. It's a pretty quiet and private place."

And he's right. It really is quite pleasant. She can hear birdsong but there is almost no sound from cars on the street. All the time she's lived here and she hasn't taken advantage of this peace and quiet. What a waste. She relaxes into her chair. When Jack says they've never been properly introduced and that his name is Jack Ford she says, "I'm Angela Wilcox." And she finds it easy to smile.

"Wilcox. Any relation to Robert Wilcox of Wilcox Industries?"

"Robert was my late husband."

"Wait . . . WHAT? Your late husband was a billionaire and you live in a boardinghouse?"

This is what she's been afraid of. You let down your guard, someone is friendly and you let yourself be friendly back, and they want to know things about you that you don't want to discuss. She says, "It's a rather long and tedious story."

"I've got nothing but time, and a friendly ear."

Her first instinct is to stand up and leave. Coming out here was a mistake. She's always kept herself to herself and she should have gone on doing it. But then . . . She's never really talked about what happened to put her here. Perhaps it's time she did. And talking to a relative stranger might be the best way to do it. She says, "There was a problem with his will. When his first wife died, he changed it to leave everything including Blythewood—that was our home—to his children. When we married, he changed it again."

"Then what . . . ?"

"He never signed it. It was never witnessed or filed. It was never made legitimate. He fell ill and died quickly before completing the process."

She can feel his fury at the injustice from where she sits. "Surely you have some recourse!"

"Our attorney managed to arrange a small monthly stipend for me, and that's what I live on. But most of the estate went to his eldest son, with a generous inheritance for his younger son."

"Don't his children have *some* familial obligation to help you out?"

"Well, his eldest son is the one who now lives on the estate and he never much cared for me. Always thought I was trying to replace his mother. He thought I was too young for his father ... that I was a 'gold digger.' So he has no intention of giving me any part of the estate. His brother, Jon, is completely different. Always offering to help. His mother died shortly after he was born so he never really knew her. We meet regularly for dinner. He's grown into a good man." Does it feel better to be getting these things off her chest? She rather thinks it does. She says, "I know this house from my childhood, so this is where I came. I didn't think I'd be here for so long. I just never bothered to leave. My mother knew Bob's aunt and I often stayed here while my mother worked. When I needed somewhere to stay, I knew Bob would take me in." She gives him a sideways look. "He has a thing for taking in wayward souls."

She'd at least half expected a reply to that, but Jack clearly hasn't understood that she includes him among the wayward souls. Perhaps she'll have to ask a more direct question. Jack says, "This is not your accustomed lifestyle."

"It's not the lifestyle I became accustomed to for a while. My mom worked all her life after my dad died. I grew up not far from here. Did well in school, went to college, landed a marketing job at Wilcox Industries. Worked my way up to executive level, met Robert. After his wife died, he needed someone to take over organizing fundraising events as she had done and it turned out I was good at that. We worked together closely on some of his pet projects and eventually it just made sense to get married."

"That's quite a story."

"It was a wonderful time. I loved him and I loved Blythewood. And I had the resources to do so much good for so many. I brought up Jon as my own son and I love him dearly." She tells him about the work she had done, the charities they supported, the galas hosted at Blythewood, the property restoration projects she had supervised, the places she'd traveled to and the people she'd met. Once she's started, the flow seems unstoppable. And then, inevitably, the backlash when she realizes she has probably spoken more since sitting down here than in the previous twelve months. "Oh my goodness," she says. "I do believe I have bored you to death!" But the fact is, it feels good to have let go of it all—as though a burden has fallen from her.

Jack says, "That was quite a data-dump. I'm glad to know more about you. And I'm honored that you are prepared to share so much with me."

"Then I invite you to return the compliment. I've said quite enough about me—what brings you to this place?" She glances at the gold Rolex on his wrist. "I get the impression you're used to better lodging yourself."

She can see him reflecting. Is he wondering whether to tell her the truth? Or what kind of distortion he might be able to get away with? But it seems he's prepared to be as open as she has been, because he says, "I'm tracking down a recently discovered relative. This house was the only long-term rental in the neighborhood. What's your plan for tomorrow? I was thinking I might check out a local concert in the park. There are flyers for it all over town. Care to join me?"

She hasn't failed to notice how quickly he changed the subject. A recently discovered relative? Discovered how? And how recently? And just how close is this relative? But, if he doesn't want to tell her those things now, she can wait. Does she want to go with him to a concert in the park? And she realizes that she does. That she may actually be starting to like this man who came, it seems, out of nowhere. And, when you come right down to it, what else does she have to do? Yet another fruitless job search? Indoors in the library, when she could be outside enjoying the fresh air and listening to music? "Yes," she says. "I think that might be quite nice."

*　　*　　*

Next morning, Angela wakes with an unusual feeling. It takes her a moment to recognize it. It's optimism. She's had it before, but not for quite a while. It's still cautious, but unquestionably there. She slips out of bed and peers through the window. The sun is shining, there's a slight breeze, it looks like a perfect day.

When was she last at a concert? She can't remember. And an outdoor concert is even harder to recall. This just might be a nice day. She rummages through her canvas closets. Way in the back of one, she finds an ankle-length linen dress in navy blue with shell buttons and long sleeves. She also digs out navy flats with gold buckles. That should do for a concert in the park. She showers, dresses, pulls up her hair, and puts on makeup. Then she practically skips down the steps to the dining room.

Waltzing into the room, she realizes no one else is there. Good grief. What time can it be?

Wendy emerges from the kitchen pulling on a fresh white apron, a beam on her face. "Bright and early this morning! How nice to see you!"

"Oh dear—I appear to be incredibly early! Are you ready to serve yet?"

"We will be shortly. Cook is prepping for breakfast now. I could get you some tea while you wait?"

"Wendy, that would be lovely."

Wendy goes back to the kitchen and comes out with tea service for Angela. "Anything special planned this morning?"

"I'm going to a concert in the park. Haven't been to a concert—or any cultural event—in so long."

"How nice! Going with anyone in particular?"

"Oh, well, Mr. Ford invited me."

"That is wonderful! But, if you don't mind me saying so, I'm not sure that dress will be very comfortable?"

Angela is surprised at Wendy's frankness, but realizes the young woman is right. The dress is a bit stiff; if she sits all day on the ground in it, it will become a wrinkled mess. "Oh dear. I suppose you're right . . ."

"No problem! I have a few minutes before breakfast service—let's pop up to your room and see what else might work!" Wendy pulls off her apron and lays it carefully over the back of Angela's dining chair so as to not crease it.

Wendy's visits to Angela's room have been few. She helped Bob clean it out, paint the walls, and scrub the floor when they needed to get it ready for its new occupant. It's hard to believe that that dingy, dusty attic has been transformed into a fresh, airy room. And Angela has filled it with things from her previous life. They rummage through the closets and drawers together. Wendy says, "Perhaps something less fussy? Something soft and comfortable?"

Angela pulls a pale turquoise open knit cardigan from a drawer. "I used to wear this in the garden . . ."

"Perfect! Do you have a white top to wear under it? I have just the right skirt. Hold on—I'll be right back!" She dashes out of the room, waving her hands in excitement.

Angela finds a short-sleeved white tee shirt trimmed with crocheted lace around the scoop neck, and some tan-colored flat sandals. She digs through her jewelry chest and finds small turquoise dangle earrings a slightly deeper shade than the sweater. Then she hears Wendy bounding up the stairs and bursting into the room. "Look what I have! I'm sure it will fit!" She's holding up a full-length broomstick skirt in various shades of turquoise, green, and blue, with a pop of pink. "Doesn't this look amazing with the sweater? And I guarantee this skirt will be comfortable." She winks at Angela.

It had not occurred to Angela that Wendy would offer her such a skirt—but she couldn't imagine why not. This is exactly the sort of thing Wendy wears every day. It's a style that suits her down to the ground—but dare Angela wear something so colorful, so *bohemian*? In another world, the answer would have been, "No." And yet . . . She looks at Wendy. "You don't think it's too young for me? It really is quite pretty. Do you know, it reminds me of a watercolor painting of an ocean."

Wendy says, "Try it. You'll love it. I have to get back to breakfast. When you come down I'll have a fresh pot of tea waiting for you."

Angela tugs off the linen dress, already wrinkled and limp, and lays it across her bed. She slips on the white shirt and tucks it into the waistband of the skirt. She studies herself in the mirror for a moment and untucks the shirt—it skims just above the hip. Yes. That's it. Bohemian? Colorful? So what? It matches to perfection the way she feels. The cardigan completes the outfit, along with the earrings and modest turquoise bracelet.

She pulls her hair out of the tight bun and French braids it loosely, fastening it at the end with a small silver clip. Then she rubs off some of her makeup and opts for lighter blush and pale lip color. As she walks by the mirror on her way out the door, she does a double take. She feels, and looks, ten years younger. The change stuns her. Will others notice?

She almost floats down the stairs. The dining room, empty when she left it, is now crowded and she hears the usual murmur of conversation—yet, when she enters the room, it goes quiet. As she passes each table, the occupants look up and smile at her. Feeling like a new person, she walks straight and tall through the room. As she approaches her table, Jack is already seated at his. When he sees her, he rises slowly out of his chair. He looks mesmerized. Is everything all right? Has she got it wrong? Is she making a fool of herself?

But Jack is beaming. He says, "Good morning. You . . . you look . . . you look amazing."

That's all right then. Astonishingly, amazing is what she feels. What has happened to the Angela of the last few months? She says, "Thank you," and reaches for the tea pot. As Wendy had promised, it's hot and fresh.

They chat over breakfast about various topics she would normally have considered frivolous. If she's honest with herself, she's feeling just the slightest bit nervous. Is this a "date"? Or does Jack just not want to go on his own? It's difficult to imagine, given the number of things he must have done alone in his life. Has he a family? He never speaks of one. Why would he come here to find a long-lost relative?

They finish their meals. As they make for the door, Jack whispers something to Wendy that Angela can't decipher, but Wendy nods and disappears into the kitchen. A moment later she's back with a picnic basket. Jack says, "We may as well make a day of it with a picnic lunch."

Well, that was thoughtful. "What a wonderful idea. How did you manage it?"

"Apparently Cook has a soft spot for people who truly appreciate her culinary skills."

As they walk toward the front entry, Jack picks up a blanket and umbrella he has left by the door. He thinks of everything. Even with her record as an organizer, Angela is impressed.

The summer's oppressing heat is over and there's a slight breeze. The sun shines happily in a sky dotted with a few fluffy white clouds. The parched grass and plants seem to be rebounding with relief.

Jack hops down the front steps in his usual way with the energy of a much younger man. Angela meets him at the bottom and they walk toward the park together. It strikes Angela that she rarely goes anywhere other than the library and Jon's apartment. And it does feel strange after all this time to be walking with another person. Strange, and somehow comforting. And there's something exciting about heading to a different destination.

Jack has done his homework and knows the best route to the park. When they arrive, people are just starting to gather, milling about the park looking for the best places to sit. Jack scopes out a perfect spot under a tree, in line of sight to the stage. He opens the blanket and unfurls it in the air with the flair she's beginning to recognize as his trademark. As it floats to the ground, he sets the basket on one corner and the umbrella off to the side within easy access. Angela curls up on one end, which is when she realizes that, for all his enthusiasm, there are some things Jack can't do as easily as he might once have done them. Watching him get on his hands and knees and then flip himself over onto the blanket makes her wonder when he last sat on the ground.

"Phew . . ." He wipes the sweat off his brow with a handkerchief. She doesn't mean to giggle, but her amusement must be obvious. She has enough experience of men to know that some of them don't like it one little bit when a woman laughs at them, however sympathetic the laugh may be. But it seems that doesn't apply to Jack because he takes one look at her face and bursts out laughing. "Been a while! Apparently this old body doesn't bend the way it used to!"

*   *   *

This has been a bit of a risk for Jack. He has no idea how good—or how bad—the community all-volunteer orchestra might be. And what Angela told him about her previous life suggests that she has probably attended concerts by some of the most prestigious symphony orchestras in the world, so she might find this a bit of a "hick" occasion. But, as it turns out, the orchestra is not at all bad. They play a variety of classical favorites, nothing too ambitious or unusual. Watching her, he can see that Angela is not passing negative judgements.

Like him, she probably finds that it's simply nice to enjoy live music.

The intermission comes and Jack pulls the picnic basket between them. "Care for some lunch?"

"How lovely! What's in here?" She lifts the basket lid and pulls back the red and white checked cloth.

"I honestly couldn't say. I asked Cook to make a nice picnic lunch and I left it to her to come up with something amazing." And I gave her a generous tip, he thinks, but didn't mention that when he said she had a soft spot for people who truly appreciate her culinary skills and there's no need to bring it up now.

He watches Angela pull out and carefully open several generous-sized containers and sees that Cook has not let him down. There's a chicken salad with red grapes, apples, and walnuts accompanied by a crusty baguette. Side dishes include a tomato and cucumber salad, a bean and pasta salad with artichokes, chopped green beans, and fresh basil, along with slices of avocado, and black olives. Cubed watermelon and sliced peaches make for a sweet and refreshing finish. He pops open the bottle of sparkling apple juice and pours some into two champagne flutes. "Not champagne, but it'll do for a toast. Here's to you and a wonderful day."

She taps his glass with hers and takes a sip. Is she blushing? He thinks she might be and he finds that sweet. Softening Jack's heart has never been difficult and Angela has done it. What makes that remarkable is that he knows she didn't intend such a thing. She spoons the lunch delicacies onto two plates and they eat quietly. He leans back against the tree and feels the sun's warmth filtering through its leaves. Has he ever felt this relaxed? This content? This kind of simple pleasure is a stranger to him and he never realized how satisfying such things could be. When he started on this journey, he thought only of the person he was searching for and never imagined meeting anyone else about whom he would feel as protective—as fond—leave it there, he tells himself; don't use any stronger word—as he does about Angela.

Everything comes to an end including the things you hate and the things you enjoy. And so, after a second half that is as good as the first, the concert is over and it's time to head home. They pack the dishes and containers into the basket, and Jack rolls up the blanket. "Do you think you could carry the umbrella? We didn't need it after all." She picks it up and they leave the park at a leisurely pace.

As they walk, Jack says, "You mentioned that you go to the library every day to check the daily papers?"

"I do. It's become my routine."

"You know I'd be happy to share my paper with you. There's no need to hurry to catch a bus to the library *every* day."

The old Angela, which is to say the Angela who ruled the roost until yesterday evening, raises her head. Just what is his game? And then she relaxes. It's just a newspaper. No harm in that. "Thank you. That would save me a couple of days of bus fare."

"Wonderful!" She half expects him to say something else, but he doesn't. When they get back to the house, she thanks him for a lovely day and goes to her room to clean up and have a little rest. And then it's time for dinner. She feels a little awkward that they are still sitting at separate tables, but what to do? If she suggests sharing the table, other people might think they've become an item. And not just other people—he might think it, too. And he doesn't seem to mind; he sits at his table and continues to make small talk while they eat. And she can't deny that this feels like being back to normal and that it's a relief. It's been a lovely day. He is a much more thoughtful person than she had imagined. But a day in the park listening to a concert is all it was.

When the meal is over and Jack invites her to sit in the backyard with him, she declines. "I'm back at it in the morning, so I think I'll turn in early. But thank you. And thank you for a day I really enjoyed. I'll see you in the morning."

"I'll be here!"

*   *   *

Next morning, when Angela reaches the dining room, Jack has been up early enough to collect his morning papers, separate out the sections he wants to study, and leave the employment section neatly folded at Angela's table. She says, "Thank you, Jack. I appreciate it."

"Now you don't have to get on that awful bus today!"

"Well, I suppose not . . ."

"Great! I was thinking of working here myself. I have some ideas to sketch, so I was planning to work right here for the day."

"I'm sure Wendy will clear a work space for you. I'll take these up to my room so I can spread them out. Thank you again." She finishes her tea, picks up the papers, and leaves the room.

Jack knows himself well and one of the things he knows is that he can be a little forward. He's begun to know Angela—at least well enough to sense that being a little forward may not appeal to her. So he smiles and lets her go. And that's the last he sees of her until dinner, at which she is cordial, she makes conversation, and Jack is content.

When he first arrived at this house, he didn't expect to stay long. Perhaps a few days; maybe a couple of weeks. He's never in the past enjoyed a slow pace of life and he hadn't expected to enjoy it now. And he certainly hadn't thought he would meet someone like Angela. The wish to leave has disappeared.

*   *   *

Angela's intention had been to go to her room and read Jack's paper there, but when she approaches the stairs Bob calls out to her. "Message for you, Angela. From . . ." He peers at the note in front of him. "From Heather?"

"Oh. What does she say?"

"Something about Jon's suggestion and how she thinks it's a great idea and she'll pick you up at ten."

"Oh. Well, thank you."

Nothing about "is this convenient for Angela?" Nothing about "let's organize something that suits us both." Just, "I'll pick you up at ten." As though she—Angela—should expect to be at Heather's beck and call. She can't say it's a surprise. Jon loves this woman and wants to marry her, so Angela will do everything in her power to smooth the way. She is about to add to that the thought that she can't pretend to like Heather, and then she realizes that pretending to like Heather is exactly what she does do when she meets her and what she will do again today. Someone should have told Heather long ago that other people are every bit as important as she is, but really that was a job for her parents and if they haven't done it Angela is certainly not going to step into the breach and play their role for them.

Bob says, "I tried to tell her you'd probably be going to the library today, but she said you wouldn't want to go to a dusty old library when you could spend a day planning her wedding with her."

Yes, Angela could see that Heather would say something like that. She could also see that Heather would think it was true. Well—look on the bright side. What she wants most of all is to make Jon's life as happy as possible and, sad though it may be, it seems that that includes being nice to the woman he plans to marry, however Angela happens to feel about her. She says, "I'll be in my room. I'll come down just before ten."

*   *   *

The car Heather had arrived in was a low-slung European sports car. Cars are of little interest to Angela and if anyone had asked her afterward the make and model, she could not have answered. What she could have said was that it was extremely close to the ground and getting into it was a feat for a contortionist. Nevertheless, getting into it was something she had to do because Heather took one look at Beauregard and said, "Angela. We can't discuss anything here. It would kill any spark of creativity either of us might have. How can you bear to live in a place like this?"

Bob heard every word and Angela looked an apology in his direction but Bob was grinning while he shook his head. He said to her afterward, "Anyone who talks like that about my house is a person I don't want here, so the fact that she wants to go somewhere else suits me down to the ground." But that was later. First came the drive, agonizing to Angela who was bent double in what Heather assured her was a racing driver's seat, and then on the other side of town an elevator ride from an underground parking garage to a gym on the fifth floor of a building that seemed to be made out of aluminum piping and panels that might have looked at home on a space shuttle.

Heather ordered cold drinks for both of them without asking what Angela would like. "It's ionized," she said. "Extremely good for you, you know. And it contains bacteria harvested from humans. So it makes your digestion work better."

"Bacteria?" Angela's stomach flipped.

"Healthy bacteria, Angela. Not all bacteria are bad for you, you know. You should keep a case of this at home. One bottle a day can work wonders. Better than a martini, I promise you that."

Angela didn't think it worth saying how long it had been since she'd last drunk a martini. "Now," said Heather. "First, this." And she took an envelope from a pocket—she didn't seem to carry a purse—and passed it across the table.

"What's that?"

"It's your fee for today, Angela. As my wedding adviser."

"But you're marrying my own stepson. I couldn't . . ."

"Yes, Jon said that's what you'd say. And I understand. I told him you'd see it as an honor you were doing us. Which, of course, it is. But he insisted that you must be paid for what you do. It's his money, it isn't mine. So, please, put it away. Now, let's talk favors."

This meeting lasted three hours, at which point Heather said, "Oh, my, I'm supposed to be at the tennis club in ten minutes. Let's adjourn and meet again next Tuesday. Angela, would you think me a beast if I asked you to make your own way home?"

A beast? Angela had actually been relieved not to have to get into that car again. She said, "Not at all, Heather. And if you let me know where you want to meet next Tuesday, I'll get myself there and you won't need to waste time picking me up."

"Oh, that would be a great help. This morning was great— I'll think about your ideas and I'm sure after we meet a couple of more times you'll get the hang of what I want. This must be the event of the year!" She jumped up and kissed the air beside Angela's cheek. "See you Tuesday." And she was gone.

Angela was tickled by the idea that she had given Heather ANY ideas because her experience had been that she'd struggled to get a word in edgewise. Every idea (and, in her view, many of them were far from "great") had come from Heather. And interspersed with those ideas had been some of the nastiest, cattiest comments about other people she'd ever heard. But at least she wasn't going to have to fold herself like a slice of New York pizza to get into that ridiculous motorized roller skate in order to find her way home. She opens the envelope containing the money Jon had sent for her. Five twenties. Good heavens. She goes to the counter. "Would it be possible for someone to call me a cab?"

CHAPTER 8

Over the next few weeks, Angela starts to become accustomed to Jack. He always has something interesting to talk about and he's generous with his time and attention. And not just with her, but with everyone he meets. She can see Wendy adores him and Bob appears to have found a fast friend. Angela has encountered charisma in the past in the life she used to lead and she knows that's what she's looking at in Jack. And not just her; the other tenants always seem entertained when they talk to him.

But an air of mystery still hangs about him. He's told her he came here to look for a long-lost relative, but not a word about whether he's found the person yet or even who the person might be. Angela assumes that most people have some mystery or secret and it isn't her place to pry. In everything else he seems so open. When he's ready, perhaps she'll learn all about it.

For herself, she still follows her own routine more often than she does not and she knows this is more about affirming her independence than anything else. Still, she makes some changes. She doesn't hurry as much as she used to. Her confining suits and tightly bound hair gradually give way to more comfortable and casual attire, even including occasionally borrowing a skirt from Wendy. She now pulls her hair back in a loose chignon, and lets Wendy make her a long, loose French braid. From time to time she joins Jack in the evening, in the garden or sometimes on the front porch swing. His conversation becomes more animated as they grow to know each other. He overflows with ideas he is bursting to share.

Once in a while, Jack surprises her with flowers, and on weekends she sometimes goes with him to the bookstore, to the park, or for lunch at a little café. He seems to enjoy such simple things. Things she never really thought about, but now realizes she enjoys as well. She feels more relaxed than she has in a long time. Her frenetic pace slows and she no longer sees living at the boardinghouse as undesirable but inevitable. She sees Jack finding interest and pleasure in everything, and being around his joyful and positive disposition makes her see the old and familiar from new perspectives. She realizes she has more than many people have—a roof over her head, good meals, enough money to get by, and people around her who care about her. While she still yearns for the life she has lost, she begins to appreciate the one she has and to learn how to make the best of it.

*   *   *

On days when Angela insists on visiting the library or doing something on her own, Jack installs himself at the coffee shop to work. Kara has chalked him up as a new regular and pours his coffee as soon as he walks in. She doesn't want to get too used to him. There's something off about this eccentric stranger showing up out of nowhere and parking himself so often in her shop. He tips a little too much, which makes her cautiously curious more than anything. He's always very pleasant with her, but it's possible to be too pleasant, and sometimes when she catches him studying her she feels a little unnerved, though she thinks he's probably harmless. She avoids his efforts at small talk—but then, she does that with everyone. In the last resort, as long as he pays and isn't demanding or intrusive, she doesn't care.

*   *   *

After happily sharing his newspapers with Angela for several days, one morning Jack asks why she doesn't job hunt online.

"That's why I visit the library. They have such great resources, and I use their computers."

"Ah—I see! You have no computer of your own?" Is this an opportunity?

"Well, I do. Jon, my stepson, gave me one some time ago, but I haven't used it much. It's pretty much useless until Wendy persuades Bob to connect the house to the Internet. And I'm pretty clueless about how to set it up. I left paid employment before I learned much about computers, and they seem to develop so fast."

It *is* an opportunity! "I know just the place! There's a coffee shop a few blocks from here. A nice quiet place where people let you be. Would you and your laptop care to join me there sometime? I can help you set it up."

He sees her pause, and he knows she's going through one of those moments she has when she examines his offer, looking for ulterior motives. He doesn't blame her; it's something he does himself, although he is far more likely to take a chance on someone than Angela is. But she surprises him: "Okay. May as well. Winter will be coming soon and slogging to the library in the cold and snow will be tiresome."

"Very good! Shall we start in the morning?"

"Um . . . sure. Okay . . . Why not? Yes—let's!"

He goes to bed that night thinking that one more bridge on the way to winning her confidence has been crossed. And he edges his way around the thought that has tried to attract his attention for some time now. He came here to find someone and he realized—with something of a shock—that the someone he came to find is Kara. Jack has always been a man of action. In the past, once he'd identified the person he was looking for he'd have lost very little time in introducing himself. Oh, sure, he'd have thought about the best way to do it and that might have taken a day or two, but it would have been done within the week. And here he is, putting it off and putting it off. Why is he doing that? Could it conceivably be the knowledge that, once he's introduced himself to Kara, he will have no reason to stay here? No reason . . . Let's be frank; no reason to maintain contact with Angela?

There. The thought is out in the open. And, as he has done before, he hastens to push it back into the dark. He's just not ready to think about that yet.

*   *   *

Angela, too, goes to bed with a feeling of satisfaction, though in her case it's because she has always felt a little guilty not to be using the laptop Jon gave her. She checks that everything is there, plugs the laptop in to charge, ready for the morning, and places it on her dressing table. When she pushes the power button, it starts to hum and the screen lights up. She switches it off again, leaves it charging, and curls up in bed with a book. Eventually, she falls asleep.

Next morning she wakes early, refreshed after a long night's sleep. She glances over to the dressing table and remembers the charging laptop. Did she make a mistake, accepting Jack's help with it? If she really wanted to use it, wouldn't she have learned to ages ago? She sighs as she pulls herself out of bed. He just wants to help. Is just being friendly. Why? Because that's how he is. Not just with her—with everyone. She showers, dresses, and goes downstairs.

She is first in the dining room. Wendy bursts through the kitchen doors, exuberant as ever. "I'll have your tea up in a jiffy!" She's back with tea almost as soon as Angela has sat down. "Whole grain toast, as usual?"

"You know, I'm feeling a bit hungry this morning. I think I'll have something a bit more. Could Cook scramble an egg with that toast?"

"She absolutely can! I'll have that right out for you!" Turning around, she almost collides with Jack as he waits to slide into his seat. "Oh! Mr. Ford! I'm so sorry!"

Jack takes a couple of steps backward with his hands in the air, slightly bumping the table behind him. "No, no—my fault. I should know to give you more room when you're in full breakfast mode."

Wendy giggles and scurries away to get the coffee pot to fill his cup, as well as the cups of the other tenants trickling into the dining room.

Jack beams. "Good morning! Fine day isn't it!"

"Yes—yes it is."

"Are you ready for our adventure today?"

"Adventure?"

"Working on your computer!"

"Oh, yes. Yes—I guess I didn't consider it an adventure."

"I consider *everything* an adventure."

Yes, she supposes he does. He really does have an enjoyment and enthusiasm for life.

Their breakfast is unusually quiet. Jack rambles on as ever but Angela, preoccupied, just nods. Part of her dreads spending the day with Jack, while another part sees no harm in it. Does she feel trapped? A little, perhaps—but she can think of no good reason not to let Jack help her. And Jack notices. "Everything okay? You seem distracted."

"Mm? Oh, no. Just some things on my mind."

"Well . . . I hope once we get you on track, it will be one less thing to worry about." He leans over and she feels a sense of shock when he puts his hand on hers. "Go grab your laptop and I'll meet you at the front door. It'll be fine. Don't worry." He can be incredibly kind, but she gently pulls back her hand as she stands.

Coming down the staircase, she sees Jack at the front door, rocking on his feet, ready to go. He looks up and grins, and somehow the grin reassures her.

*   *   *

It's later than Jack's usual time when they enter the coffee shop and the morning rush is in full swing. Kara looks up and sees Jack with someone—a woman no less. In fact, an attractive, classy-looking woman. That's good—she won't have to put up with his stares. "What can I get you?"

"Good morning!" Oh, that beam—she hates the way he beams. Does he do it just for her or does everyone get the full multi-megawatt charge? Who cares? She doesn't like it. He says, "I'll have my usual, and my friend will have . . ." And he turns to look at Angela.

"Tea. Hot tea will be fine."

"Got it—give me a sec." She spins round to grab a couple of cups. She puts one on the counter and fills it with coffee, leaving room for milk. The other she places on a saucer along with a wrapped teabag and fills the cup with hot water. "Anything else?"

"That will do for now. Thanks so much." He hands her a twenty-dollar bill. "Keep our tab running, will you?"

"Yeah, sure, sure. I'll 'run a tab.'" She rolls her eyes. What kind of stage show does this guy think he's been cast in?

*   *   *

They go to Jack's regular table. Angela, her executive background waking up, says, "For a customer-facing position, she isn't the most gregarious person."

"Oh, she's all right. She keeps a tidy shop."

She takes her laptop out of its case. Compared with Jack's, which has clearly seen better days and is more than a little beat up, it's slender and light. She is sure Jon took its weight into consideration when choosing it for her. When she presses the power button it comes on, fully charged and ready to go. Jack shows her how to connect to the shop's Internet and set up a browser. She is stunned. She can do everything she wants on her own, at practically anytime. Jack uses a free webmail service to set up an email address for her. "Now you can apply for positions online, which is what people want these days. An awful lot of applications sent by mail are thrown in the trash without even being read."

She sees that Jack was right about Kara. She does keep the shop clean and tidy. Not very conversational but efficient, hard-working, and in constant motion. It's a quaint little coffee shop and she can see how Jack might think it charming. But she doesn't care for Kara's way of making tea. Good tea requires that the leaves come into contact with freshly boiling water and remain that way for a few minutes. But there you are—most of America doesn't seem to know that. No wonder tea has never really become popular on this side of the Atlantic.

And so, then and over the following days, Angela masters the use of her laptop. She sees a whole world of information and communication opening to her and wonders why she waited so long to embrace technology. Jack has made it seem so easy. She thinks back to the first time she met him and wouldn't give him the time of day, let alone sit with him in a coffee shop, letting him teach her anything. Now she goes with him to places where they can both work—the coffee shop, the bookstore, the local community center for an occasional change—and it beats taking a bus to the library.

There are other benefits. Being introduced to things she had never noticed even after living here for so long, she finds herself worrying less and less about her own circumstances. She doesn't give a thought to what will happen when Jack's stay at the house comes to an end. And then comes the invitation to dinner with Jon and Heather.

"I'll see you when you get back?" Jack asks that afternoon as they stroll back to the house after visiting a small art gallery newly opened in an old firehouse.

"I'm not sure—these evenings tend to run a bit late. I really don't know what to expect with Heather there." She's not looking forward to the evening because the subject at her last meeting with Heather had been where the wedding should take place. She knows what Heather wants, she knows she probably can't have it, she's fairly sure that Jon's reaction to the idea will be negative, and she's already seen enough of Heather to know how she acts when things don't go her way. But what can she do? And the question of location is going to have to be settled soon— should, in fact, already have been settled because the best places for any kind of function including a wedding get booked up well in advance, though Heather doesn't seem to understand that. As far as she's concerned, if she wants a place on a date when it's already booked by someone else, the someone else will have to find another venue. And smile while they're doing it.

"Not to worry. I'll wait up in the front room. Just to make sure you get in okay."

She knows she should be infuriated by the level of presumption in that remark, but although she won't show it she's secretly pleased that he cares enough to watch out for her. "It isn't necessary. But it would be nice to not walk alone into a dark house."

"Have a wonderful time and I look forward to hearing all about it later."

CHAPTER 9

J on answers the door in his usual casual way. "Ange! I'm so glad you're here!" He hugs her tight.

"Hello, my love. Is Heather joining us tonight?"

"She's on her way. Rushing around, no doubt, doing whatever it is she does."

"What does that mean?"

"Well, you know. Being a trust-fund baby, she wouldn't know what it means to *work*." Jon laughs. "I'm hoping you'll be a good role model for her and she'll find some charitable causes she cares about and throw herself into something meaningful."

"I'm not too sure about that ... Is Heather the philanthropic type?"

There's something a little uneasy in Jon's laugh. "Perhaps it's something you can grow into." He puts his hands on Angela's shoulders and steps back. "Hey, Ange, you're glowing! What's up?"

Angela blushes. "Oh . . . I think I'm finally allowing my life to unfold rather than trying to force it. I think I'm finding peace."

"WOW—that's wonderful! You know you always have a place here—with me. But if you're happy, then that's wonderful. Could there be a *reason* you're happier ... ?"

Being asked the question forces her to think about the answer. And then to think about how much of the answer she wants to share. "Well ... an interesting person has been staying at the house. It turns out he's quite nice."

"ANGE! That's great!"

"You know I still miss your father ..."

"I know you do. But he's gone and you have a lot of life ahead of you. And whether you like it or not, he did let you down. Oh yes he did, so take that look off your face. What matters is how you are now. If you're happy, I'm happy."

He pulls her in for another hug and Angela feels once again how fortunate she is to have such a wonderful young man in her life. "So," she says, "what's on the menu tonight?"

"I thought I'd dabble with some Thai chicken and noodles. I was thinking lettuce wraps? Pretty basic really. What do you think?"

"Sounds wonderful. I'm starved."

They head to the kitchen and Jon takes a bottle of wine from the refrigerator and pours a glass each. He raises his glass. "A toast—to happiness!"

Before they have a chance to sip their wine, the front door bursts open and Heather bounces in. Tall and slim with wide hips, Heather's bleached blonde hair with dark roots is piled high on her head in a messy bun. Her bright floral leggings in shades of hot pink, turquoise, and yellow are topped with a neon yellow hip-length zipped jacket from which a hot-pink sports bra peeks out under the top of the zipper. Her bronze skin hints at a tanning session that day. Her makeup is a little overdone for Angela's taste; her neon pink lipstick matches her sports bra and her acrylic nails are a glittery pink. Her white sneakers are spotless. She still carries no purse, but has a mobile phone in her hand. "Oh my gosh—you wouldn't *believe* the *darling* little frames I just found and we can get them monogrammed and put our pictures in them and give them to everyone as wedding favors! So they will NEVER forget OUR special day! Sweetie— just look at these!" She squeals as she shoves her phone in Jon's face.

Her voice rasps when she speaks and it always sounds like she needs to clear her throat. Practically every sentence ends in a rising intonation, making everything she says sound like a question. Angela can't help finding her voice and her manner of speaking grating, but hopes she'll get used to it. And it's clear Jon doesn't mind. And, after all, she doesn't have to hear it on a daily basis.

Jon gently guides the phone down and away from his face. "Hi, Heath. Angela's here. Why don't we look at them after dinner?" He kisses her lightly on the cheek. "And I'm not sure everyone that comes to the wedding will really want *our* picture in a frame with *our* initials."

"OH! I didn't even SEE you there! Hi, Angela." Heather reaches out and takes Angela's hand in her own and practically pulls her into the conversation.

Quite how anyone could miss two people standing directly in front of her in Jon's small kitchen is a puzzle to Angela. Must have been Heather's excitement. "Hello, Heather. It's so nice to see you again."

Heather's smile is sweet. Too sweet? But Heather leads her to the couch, practically pushes her to sit, and plops down beside her, a bit too close for someone she barely knows. She has a captive audience and chats incessantly while Jon sets out their meals on the dinner table.

"Come and get it!" Jon calls.

Angela is relieved to move away from Heather and rise from the couch. "Jon—this looks delicious."

Heather bounces to the table and grimaces. "Ohhhhhhh, sweetie. I have water aerobics in the morning. I'll be all bloated if I eat this. Do you have a salad?"

Angela listens in silence. Did she really see a pout on Heather's face? And if Heather has special dietary needs this evening, why didn't she mention them earlier? Like, when Jon was still planning what to give them to eat? Wouldn't that have been the thoughtful thing to do?

"Sorry—I didn't know. I don't have much . . . let's see."

They rummage through his kitchen and Heather decides some fruit would be fine. She takes an apple and a peach out of the crisper drawer, plops them on a plate, and takes them to the table with a paring knife. The advantage of Heather's meager meal—for Heather—is that it gives her more space to talk. And Angela always feels that Heather could talk for America. Angela and Jon barely get a word in while Heather rambles on about the latest battle with her bridesmaids over what style of dress she wants them to wear and switches without a pause to her new workout schedule. She pulls up pictures on her phone of hairstyles, nail treatments, and elaborate multi-tier cakes.

Angela becomes breathless wondering how to keep up with her . . . or rein her in. She also notices that everything Heather says is about the wedding. There's no mention of where they will live afterward, whether they will have children, what she'll do after they are married, or what plans they have discussed for their life together. She's asked this before at more than one of their meetings, but Heather has always ignored the question. Perhaps now she can get some input from Jon. As casually as possible, she asks, "Where do you think you'll live when you're married?"

Heather gestures around Jon's apartment. "Well—I assume we'll live here . . . for now. Of course I'll want a big, beautiful home eventually." Heather throws up her arms indicating a huge house. "I have so many decorating ideas! This place is just too 'bachelor pad' to do anything with. I need a big, new house to do what I want with!"

Angela sees Jon stifling a wince. Really, noticing that should be the fiancée's job, but Heather seems oblivious to what other people are thinking. He says, "Babe. I don't make a whole lot with my work. It will be some time before we are ready for a house."

"Oh come on! With your inheritance, you probably don't even *need* to work! I know you do the photo thing just to stay busy. I'm sure your father left you enough for a house socked away somewhere."

Angela can see Jon growing more and more uncomfortable.

"Heath, I do the work I do because I enjoy it and it gives me an opportunity to give back. Just the other day, I was asked to take some shots for a children's hospital for their fundraising campaign—"

"That's nice, dear . . . But I don't imagine it pays much."

"I'm not doing it for the money. I told them I would do it for free—"

"You're kidding me, right?"

"No. I think it will be fun. I'm really looking forward to meeting the kids and touring the hospital. They have a really amazing facility. Hey . . . you could come with me! You could volunteer! I'm sure the kids would love that!"

"Well, sweetie, I just don't think I have space in my schedule for any . . . *volunteering*. Especially not at a hospital. What if I get something? I can't get sick." She picks up her phone and starts swiping through images of centerpieces of fish bowls complete with goldfish, hand-painted porcelain wedding favor boxes, and wedding cake–shaped piñatas. "Hey, sweetie, should we get a photo booth for the reception? Wouldn't it be so *fun* for everyone to take goofy pictures of themselves at the reception?" Now Angela is on full alert because Heather has raised the subject of the reception and it's a very short step from there to the suggestion that is going to cause so much trouble. But Heather seems oblivious to this. She says, "Oh. And speaking of the reception—I had the most wonderful idea the other day! I suggested it to Angela but somehow we didn't seem to be on the same wavelength. Anyways, here it is: we'll have the reception at *your* house! My parents' house is being renovated and it won't be ready in time for the wedding. Wouldn't it be great to have a big party for all our friends at your estate? I think it would just be *DIVINE*. What's it called again?"

"Blythewood," says Angela.

"That's *right*. Isn't that *quaint?*"

For the first time ever on a visit to Jon's apartment, Angela has begun to wish she was somewhere else. Jon says, "Only, it isn't my house. My brother already agreed to having the engagement party at the house. *His* house. I think we need to do the wedding somewhere else."

"What better place than the childhood home of my wonderful, handsome husband-to-be? It's such a grand place for a grand event. I can think of no place better!"

"It would be a huge imposition on my brother and his wife to have our wedding there. Really, Heath, *THEY* didn't even get married there!"

"Then all the more reason why YOU should!" Heather pokes her finger into his shoulder on the last two words, then crosses her arms. "Don't you want to make your future wife happy?"

"Heather. We'll talk about this later. You're embarrassing Angela."

Heather pouts and turns to Angela, twirling a tendril of hair in her fingers as she turns her head. "Angela—don't *you* think we should have the wedding at Jon's house? Haven't I talked you round yet? I mean, really. What better place?"

"It's not my place to say, Heather. It's really up to Robert."

"Well, we'll just see about that. I'll speak to his wife . . . what was her name again? Kathy?"

Jon says, "She prefers Katherine."

"I'll give Katherine a call and see what *she* thinks. I'll bet anything *she'll* think it's a fabulous idea!" She jumps out of her seat, and picks up her phone. "I gotta go. I have a Prancercise session tomorrow morning."

Jon says, "I thought you had water aerobics?"

"Well—ye-AH. *AFTER* Prancercise, of course!"

Heather puts her cheek on Jon's, kisses the air next to his ear, and heads to the door. "OH!" Heather spins around on her toes to face Angela. "And, Angela—it would be so much easier to just send you all my great ideas. What's your email address?"

"Oh gosh—I just set it up and I don't remember. Just, uh, send them to Jon and we'll figure it out."

"How could someone not know their email address? Oh—well—okay." She snorts and bolts out the door, slamming it behind her.

The feeling in the room is like the calm after the storm. Jon says, "She's a handful. But she means well . . . right?"

"Oh sure, Jon. It'll all be fine."

But would it? Angela really doesn't think so.

CHAPTER 10

Next morning, Jack meets Angela in the sitting room and they walk together to the coffee shop. It's a beautiful day and Angela is comfortable in a light sweater and some cotton slacks she hasn't worn in years, along with some tennis shoes she found in the back of the closet. Since she isn't on the court these days, she may as well wear them to walk. She says, "Thank you again for waiting up for me last night. It really wasn't necessary."

"It was absolutely my pleasure. I was glad to see you get home safely."

This is the kind of moment that Angela feels is right for asking questions. "So . . . what is it exactly that you do? What are all the sketches? What are you always working on?"

"Well . . . I guess you could say I'm an 'inventor' of sorts."

"But what do you 'invent'?"

"Oh . . . I dabble in engines and propulsion systems."

She recognizes that that is all she's going to get right now—but it does explain his familiarity with Wilcox Industries. They arrive at the coffee shop and Jack appears pleased to see Kara. He chats her up a bit, just as she has watched him do for the last several days. She seems unimpressed and Angela doesn't give his friendliness with a waitress a second thought.

It's simply his nature—he is overly sociable with everyone, including her. They have just reached Jack's regular table when a tall, sinewy, rather rough-looking man with a scruffy beard, unkempt hair under a dirty ball cap, dirty jeans, and a heavy, dark jacket bursts into the shop and storms up to the counter. She sees Kara look up from wiping down the pastry case and rise to meet him. What they are saying can't be heard at this distance but it looks like an exchange of harsh words. Kara turns away and the man reaches over the counter and grabs her arm, pulling her back to the counter with such force that the side of her body hits the counter with a dull *thud*.

Jack is out of his chair so fast it crashes to the floor. Before he can reach the counter, the man becomes aware that everyone in the shop is watching him. He releases Kara, almost pushing her away, and storms out the door.

"Oh my goodness—I hope she's all right," whispers Angela as she leans over and puts her hand on Jack's arm. He picks up his chair and sits back at the table. She sees he is seething but he has kept control of himself. Angela says, "Why do people think they need to act so . . . uncivilized?"

"He has no right to touch her like that."

Is he more worked up over the incident than a reasonable person would expect? She chalks it up to his being a good, decent man himself and this sort of behavior being beneath him. She's a bit shaken herself. "Jack—I'm not sure I can concentrate. Shall we go for a walk and shake this off?"

"Good idea." He stands up and holds out a hand for Angela. They gather their belongings. As they head to the door, Jack pauses at the counter, letting Angela go ahead. He leans over the counter and speaks in a low voice. "Are you all right?"

"Yeah, yeah. That's nothing. You should see him when he's really mad."

"What?!!?"

"I'm fine. He'll be all right once he sleeps it off." She turns back to her work.

Jack's head is spinning. He just can't let her stay in this situation. Not if she is in danger. What if he really hurt her?

Jack knows he needs to do something about this situation with Kara, and needs to do it soon.

After a short burst of fresh air in the park, Angela decides to head back to the house and Jack says he'll check out the bookstore. They advertise free Internet and he needs an alternative to going to a coffee shop every day. "I've just about had my fill of coffee."

Walking slowly back to the house, Angela ponders what's been happening since this man—by all outward appearances a good and decent man—came to live at Beauregard. She knows from talking to him that he's well-traveled, well-read, and very clever. She just can't shake the mystery of why he is at this broken-down boardinghouse. Surely he could have found a better long-term rental. He's shown his enjoyment of and care for other people to be genuine. That has to count for something. And she can trust him. She's on the verge of a momentous decision. Whether she has the courage to make it, she has yet to discover.

*   *   *

That evening, she is—as usual—early to the dining room. Wendy bounces out of the kitchen to greet her with a tall glass of ice water with a lemon wedge on a small saucer. "Good evening, Miss Angela! Did you have a good day?"

"Thank you, Wendy. It was . . . interesting."

"Oh dear! That sounds ominous."

"A little shake-up at the coffeehouse so we called it an early day. What's on the menu tonight?"

"Herb-roasted chicken with roasted baby potatoes and petite green beans. It smells amazing in the kitchen!"

"I'm actually pretty hungry tonight." And now she is no longer on the verge of a decision—she has to make it. "I think I'll just wait for a few minutes . . ."

Then Wendy hears a sound behind her. She turns to see where it comes from. "Oh, Mr. Ford! I'll have your table ready in just a moment."

Here it is. Grasp the nettle. Or you may regret it forever. She says, "I think Mr. Ford will be joining me at my table tonight. Jack?"

"It will be my honor." He smiles and pulls out the chair across from Angela. She can't help noticing the glee on Wendy's face. Whatever can be going through the girl's mind? Well, never mind that—what might now be going through Jack's?

Wendy says, "Mr. Ford, tonight we have . . ."

"Whatever Cook makes, I'll eat." He is smiling and his eyes don't leave Angela's face.

"I'll have your dinners right out!"

Despite the upset that morning, a calmness has descended on Angela. She feels safe. She has the feeling that Jack would never let anything happen to her. This is something she hasn't felt in a long time and she's glad for it. Since she first came to live at this house, urgency and panic have been her daily companions—and now? Now life seems to have slowed down. She's begun to live each day as it comes instead of worrying about her future. She has also begun to realize just how fortunate she really is . . . she has a reliable place to live, good food and, now, good company.

Jack folds his hands on the tabletop. "Well . . . this is nice."

"I thought it foolish to go on sitting at two separate tables right next to each other. This makes conversation so much easier. Don't you agree?"

"I do. Much easier. And much more agreeable."

Wendy arrives and sets two plates of food before them. Jack says, "Wendy, this looks amazing. Give Cook my compliments." When she's gone, he says, "There's another symphony concert if you're interested. I thoroughly enjoy concerts. I think it's at the high school auditorium, if that's okay with you?"

"That would be lovely. I would enjoy that."

"Might I entice you to dinner out before the concert? I found this nice little Italian restaurant near the concert venue. I'd like to try it and it just wouldn't be the same on my own."

It seems that, once you've made one decision, others have to follow. She hasn't any doubt that this much-traveled man has often eaten on his own in restaurants and enjoyed the experience but, if he's offering it to her, why say no? "Why, yes, I think I might like that."

*   *   *

On the evening of the concert, she puts on a pale apricot A-line dress with dyed-to-match lace bolero jacket and neutral beige kitten-heels and clutch. It's years since she wore her pearl necklace and earrings, but she feels they are exactly right for the occasion. Her hair is pulled back loosely at the sides and cascades down her shoulders and back. Jack waits at the bottom of the stairs, handsome in a navy suit, pale blue shirt, and a tie striped with both shades. His black leather shoes are polished to a high shine. She sees him before he sees her, shuffling his feet and wringing his hands nervously like a teenager on a first date. Then he looks up. As she descends the stairs, he gasps. "You look amazing."

She blushes. She can't help herself. For so long she hasn't wanted to fix herself up, to look good . . . to *feel* good. She had resigned herself to staying in the background, anonymous, a mouse scurrying about her desperate days and retreating to her room every night. Jack has changed all that. He's made her feel special and important. She feels like she *matters* again in a way she hadn't even imagined. She reaches the bottom step and slips her arm into his as if it was the most natural thing in the world. Jack beams and opens the front door with a flourish of his hand for her to proceed. To giggle now would be completely at odds with the grown, experienced woman she is—but that doesn't stop her. She had thought giggles were a thing of the past. She was wrong.

Jack says, "It's a beautiful evening. Shall I call a car or shall we walk?"

"Oh, let's walk. I don't think it's far and pretty soon we won't have many nice evenings like this left."

Going down the front porch steps onto the walk, Angela feels supported not only by having her arm in Jack's, but also by the feeling that he would support her in whatever she wanted to do. They stroll the few blocks to a quaint Italian restaurant which is actually the ground floor of a house. Angela has never noticed this place, probably because it looks from the street like a regular home. Jack opens the front door and she is astonished by a lovely foyer with a polished, ornately carved wood podium and a shining crystal chandelier hanging above it. The young woman standing behind the podium is quite beautiful with long, wavy jet-black hair and a mid-length black lace dress with dark stockings and black shoes. Her eyes are heavily lined and she wears red lipstick with the faintest hint of blush. Her dangling earrings glitter in the light. "Good evening," she says with just a hint of an accent. "Two for dinner?"

Jack says, "Yes, please!"

She picks up two menus and leads them to a table. As they walk, Angela glances to the other side and sees a gleaming, decorated barroom with a long ornately carved bar. A mirror the length of the bar hangs on the wall behind it over dark red wallpaper. There are several small tables with a small lit candle on each and chairs with red seat cushions. She imagines couples meeting for first dates, or coming here year after year to celebrate anniversaries. She feels surprisingly good here; the place is designed to make its patrons feel comfortable and at home.

Their table is in front of the window facing the street. There are only two other couples in the small room, although there are several tables with white linen tablecloths and the same chairs with red cushions. The walls are covered in the same dark red wallpaper, and a lit candle and small bud vase with a red rose and some greens are on every table. The lighting is perfect—not too bright, but enough to see around the room. Angela finds the setting quite romantic.

The hostess leaves them with their menus. "Your waiter will be here in just a moment."

"Oh my goodness," says Angela. "This is lovely! I had no idea there was a place like this in the neighborhood."

"It is quite a find, isn't it? I heard the family moved here from Italy some years ago. They bought this broken-down house and fixed it up to open an authentic Italian cuisine restaurant."

"They certainly did that. If you didn't know where you were, you might think you actually were in Italy."

A waiter appears as if out of nowhere. Dressed in a crisp white shirt, red tie, black trousers, polished black shoes, and a white apron, he carries himself very straight, keeping his hands behind his back as he speaks. He offers to answer any questions they have about the menu and when there are none takes their order without the aid of a notepad. He reappears in a few moments with their starters of caprese salad and a bottle of prosecco. The crusty bread is still warm and easily soaks up the olive oil dressed with herbs. Angela has opted for melanzane parmigiana and Jack has ordered cioppino. He says, "I know it isn't really *Italian* Italian, but . . ."

"It isn't? I've eaten fish stews very like it in Italy."

"I know. And that's what it's based on. But it was developed in San Francisco, admittedly by Italian cooks, to suit the ingredients they found here."

When the food arrives, Angela sees with relief that the portions are not overwhelming. The eggplant is baked to perfection and the sauce so light she knows it has to be made from fresh tomatoes. Jack is pleasantly surprised at his plate brimming with salmon, shrimp, clams, mussels, and scallops on a bed of linguine with an herby, spicy seafood broth. The plates are presented beautifully and perfectly. Not a drop out of place. They finish with the tiramisu that seems obligatory in such a place. It's so light, Jack jokes that it might float off the plate.

Apart from dinners at Jon's apartment, it's so long since Angela had a meal outside the boardinghouse. There is something about dressing and dining out that no other pleasure can replace. She relishes every moment and every bite. And then they walk the few blocks to the concert.

*   *   *

The high school parking lot is full. People are milling around outside and the lobby is packed. They work their way through the crowd to a long folding table against the far wall staffed by several people with small cash boxes ready to sell tickets and take donations. Jack buys two tickets and is his ever gracious, personable self. As they start to walk away from the table and into the auditorium, he stops. "You go ahead and find good seats. I'm feeling really good tonight and I want to give them a small donation."

His generosity is one of the things Angela most likes about Jack. She pauses at the door to the auditorium and turns back to see him conversing with an extremely thin, unsmiling, balding man in a blue pinstripe suit and large wire-rimmed glasses. The man looks unimpressed with Jack's conversation as Jack reaches into his jacket pocket to pull out a checkbook. She can see he is still talking as he writes a check and hands it to the unimpressed, thin man. The man looks at the check and looks at Jack, his eyes growing wide, slowly rising out of his seat. A broad smile spreads across his face and he grabs Jack's hand and shakes it as if he is going to shake it off his shoulder. Jack slips his checkbook back into his jacket with his free hand and pats the man on the shoulder.

Jack wears a broad smile as he works his way back to Angela. She says, "What was that about?"

"Oh, nothing. I just gave him a small donation. He was just very appreciative, I guess. Now—let's go find some good seats."

The concert features Rachmaninoff's second piano concerto, performed by a well-known pianist who is in the area working with the youth orchestra. Jack suggests they sit where they can see the pianist's hands. The orchestra turns out to be quite talented and the pianist magnificent. His large hands fly and glide over the keyboard, the piano seeming to sing as if it has a voice. The second movement in particular brings tears to Angela's eyes. She has heard this piece hundreds of times before—has even sponsored concerts featuring this piece—but now, this evening, something is different. The time, the place . . . the company. She is overwhelmed by Jack's kindness and sitting in this auditorium taking in the beautiful music with him just gets the better of her. And Jack must have noticed because he lifts his hand off his lap and places it on her hand in her lap. As her tears fall, she feels the gentle support he offers as he holds her hand gently for the rest of the concert.

When the house lights come up, Angela realizes she has streaks on her cheeks from her falling tears. She wipes her face with her fingertips. Jack hands her a clean, white handkerchief from his inside jacket pocket. "Are you okay?"

"Yes, yes, oh yes. It was a beautiful concert. It's just been so long . . ." She doesn't want to go on.

"I understand." They rise from their seats.

Angela says, "My goodness. What an evening. I'm exhausted. Shall we go?"

"Of course. Let's get home." He takes her arm and leads her out of the auditorium. The slightly chilly air feels good. They walk home slowly, quietly, her arm in his. She is still glowing from a wonderful outing.

CHAPTER 11

Planning is in full swing for a spring wedding. Heather drags Angela to all sorts of appointments, venues, dress shops, bakeries, and caterers. She is obsessed with making her wedding to Jon a huge bash—the event of the year.

One particularly crisp and clear autumn day, Angela and Jon must accompany Heather to an all-day tasting and tour of an upstate winery to sample entrees, desserts and, of course, wine. The thought of spending the entire day with Heather at an event where alcohol is involved makes Angela wary, but Jon assures her he will keep things in line and that *he* will drive. One of the benefits of that is that they go in Jon's car, a sedan with enough room for Angela to be comfortable.

*　　*　　*

Meanwhile, Jack has decided to bite the bullet. Is this the perfect day to talk to Kara and reveal why he is in this place at this time? Maybe. Maybe not. But is there ever going to be a perfect time? So, if not now, when? In his head, he plays out their conversation, the questions she would ask, the answers he would provide. Every scenario ends with her throwing her arms around him and welcoming him as her father.

It's time. The day is winding down and all the other customers have left. Kara moves through the shop methodically, deliberately. She has a routine for cleaning up and closing. Jack has never really watched how she goes about her work, putting everything just so, wiping everything down, preparing for the next day. He's watching her now. And she knows it. And she's angry. "Look . . . I don't know what your deal is, but you've been hanging around here long enough. Time to go find another waitress to stare at."

"You don't understand. I'm not a stalker."

"Like hell you aren't. You come in here all moony-eyed staring at me. It's creepy."

"Kara . . . I, I . . . there's something I need to tell you."

"Yeah, right. This better be good." She throws the dishcloth on his table, folds her arms across herself, and shifts her hips.

Jack has rehearsed this in his head so many times, and this is not how he imagined it. He wasn't prepared for her defensiveness. How can he frame this? "I . . . I knew your mother."

"Sure. Okay. A lotta guys knew my mother. If you know what I mean . . . Wait—oh my God—is *that* what you mean? IS IT?"

"Well, yes, I guess . . ."

"You GUESS?!!?"

"Um, well, it turns out . . . Kara, I'm your father."

"My WHAT?!!?" Her face is bright red.

"Look, I received a letter from your mother . . ."

"My mother DIED." Her eyes well with tears.

"Yes, yes, I know and I'm sorry. She knew she was sick and sent me these letters." Jack reaches into his case and pulls out two plain white envelopes, one of which is opened. "She sent me a letter, telling me about you. She sent me your picture." He reaches into the open envelope and takes out the picture of the young girl and hands it to Kara.

Kara stares at the picture. He thinks she isn't going to speak, but then she says, "I was twelve when that was taken. Twelve. That was my birthday party. It was the best day of my life. Before Mom got sick and there weren't any more birthday parties, much less photographs. And then it was too late." She thrusts the picture back into Jack's hand.

"She told me you were in this area and asked me to find you and take care of you."

"I don't NEED taking care of! I am JUST FINE. And why didn't you try to find me sooner? Some poor excuse for an absentee father YOU are!"

In all his years of dealing with people of every type in every situation, Jack has never known a struggle to communicate like this. He doesn't know how to explain, or what to say to make it right. "I . . . I . . . didn't even know you existed until I got these letters. If I had known, I would have . . ."

"Would have WHAT?"

"Look. She sent this letter for you. She said it would explain." He hands her the second, unopened envelope. She tears it open and starts to read. Tears are rolling down her cheeks.

"Oh my God. This is her handwriting. Why didn't she tell me? Why didn't she EVER tell me? All these years I figured my dad was some one-night schmuck . . ."

"Well, actually . . ."

"You're NOT helping!"

"Sorry. I'm sorry." He raises his hands. "Look—I know this is a shock. I'm actually quite pleased how I found you." He tries a smile but shrinks back when he sees the look Kara gives him. "But—that's not important. I want to make this right. I want to make it up to you. I'm in a good position to help you—"

"HELP me?"

Jack pulls out a handkerchief and wipes the sweat off his face and forehead. "Maybe after you read her letter, we can talk? Figure this out?"

"I need to think on this. I don't know. I just don't know right now . . . I need time."

"Take all the time you need. When you're ready, we'll figure out how to move forward."

"Or not. I may decide we don't move forward AT ALL. I may decide the only moving forward I'm going to do is to bar you from this shop."

"Yes, yes, well . . . I certainly hope we can. I really want to. I don't have any other children. I want to figure this out."

"Please. Just leave. I need to finish cleaning up and get outta here."

"Okay. I understand. Here . . . here's my card with my number." He hands her a plain white business card with his name and mobile number on it. "Please keep it and call me when you're ready to talk. Please don't take too long? Maybe we can talk tomorrow?"

"Tomorrow? Are you KIDDING me? No. I don't think we'll be talking tomorrow. I need time. A lot of time . . . My life was okay. Not great, I have problems, but okay. I never expected this. I never had a father. Now I've not only got one, I've got one that actually wants to know me. I'm going to need time to take that in."

What Jack wants now more than anything in the world is to be able to reach out and hug Kara. But that isn't going to happen anytime soon because she's turned her back and walked into the back room in a signal that could not be clearer. He packs up his laptop and gathers his things. It's done. It may not have been the way he had imagined—the way he had hoped—but it's out there. She knows. The most difficult part of the task of introducing himself to his daughter has been done. And now the cards will fall as they may.

The bell on the door jingles as it closes behind him.

*   *   *

As the crisp autumn days slip into colder days of winter, Angela takes it upon herself to be the house's holiday organizer. While she's on winter break from school, Wendy is more than thrilled to become Angela's right-hand person and learn all she can from a master event planner. Resources are limited, so they have to be creative, but Angela is confident they can pull off a beautiful and magical holiday season filled with joy and celebration.

When he cleaned out the attic to make a private space for Angela, Bob didn't have the heart to throw away decades of family mementos so he boxed everything up and stored it all in the basement. With his blessing, they rummage through the dark, musty basement. Surprisingly well organized, Bob's handiwork is apparent in the way the boxes are marked and stacked neatly. They gingerly open boxes looking for anything they can use.

In one box, carefully wrapped in soft cloth, is an entire silver tea set, two silver candlesticks, and a dozen or so mismatched silver napkin holders. Angela thinks there might be just enough napkin holders for all the residents, and the remaining silver pieces could be arranged beautifully with some seasonal gourds and colored leaves from the maple trees around the house. They discover a huge platter that would present a magnificent turkey beautifully, which is when they decide to do Thanksgiving dinner family style, since they are basically a sort of family.

More discoveries await. Beautiful linens, including lace tablecloths and fine linen napkins trimmed in gold embroidery, tiny hand-hewn wooden bowls—perfect for nut cups—and a couple of ceramic pumpkins that appear to be missing their tops.

Another box holds dozens of candles. Half-burned pillar candles, brand-new tapers, tea lights—every type and size candle imaginable, some used, some new. Angela is thrilled and imagines a Christmas Eve with the dining room glowing with candlelight, but Wendy reminds her that Bob packed away all these candles years ago for safety purposes. But if a few were placed carefully and with consideration so as to not be toppled to cause a fire, they just might be able to use them for a single evening.

The two women spend hours rummaging through the treasures, so losing track of time that Bob has to come looking for Wendy to prep the dining room for the evening meal. Wendy apologizes, and Bob feigns annoyance, but Angela catches his smile behind Wendy's back as she bounds up the stairs and knows he is anything but annoyed with her. She is sure she hears him chuckle as he lumbers up the creaky ancient stairs.

They spend the next few days cleaning and prepping the rewards of their hunt. Then it's time to plan dinner. Wendy helps Angela plan a traditional dinner with consideration for any residents' dietary restrictions and to keep the meal within budget. Cook seems to be a master at making something out of nothing, and Wendy is confident that she will present an amazing Thanksgiving meal with as many trimmings as possible.

In the days leading up to Thanksgiving, Angela feels more alive than she has in months, perhaps years. Though small compared to the multimillion-dollar gala events she arranged and managed in the past, there is something relaxed, intimate, *personal* about this occasion. This is going to be unique and far more meaningful than anything she has ever done before.

Jack is pleased to see Angela doing something that truly suits her talents. The joy she takes in the holiday planning is obvious and he takes great pleasure in watching her ideas unfold. He watches her blossom with the energy of the holiday season.

Jack isn't used to celebrating holidays. He usually spent the time traveling, in a hotel room, eating dinner alone in a quiet restaurant. He never complained—it was the nature of his business, and he had no family to visit, nowhere to go. But he also didn't know what he had been missing. He finds immense joy in joining the inhabitants of this house, and especially Angela, to experience the most enchanting holiday season he has known since he was a child. It is like spending the holidays with an extremely eccentric family and he loves every minute of it.

Angela and Wendy have a glorious time rummaging around the backyard finding brilliantly colored leaves, acorns, and other tidbits to use in their displays. Closing down for the winter, the local farmer's market gives Angela a deal on gourds and pumpkins. They spend the day before Thanksgiving decorating the dining room, displaying their special finds.

Some of Bob's pieces just seem to fit perfectly in the house and Angela thinks they should never have been hidden away. She tells herself Bob most likely did so to prevent them being lifted by the occasional "outside" boarder, but that isn't a risk over the holidays and she promises herself she'll pack everything she has borrowed just as she found them. Bob has done so much for her, and while he seems pretty nonchalant about letting her go through those boxes, she wants to return his kindness and support. She still has no other place to go, so she needs to respect that this is his house and she is staying here at a token rate.

After breakfast on Thanksgiving morning, Wendy and Angela put all the tables together in one big row down the middle of the dining room as dinner will be served family style. They lay overlapping tablecloths diagonally down the row of tables, and roll napkins into the silver napkin rings. They create several centerpieces using the ceramic pumpkins with sprigs of leaves, along with the gourds and pumpkins from the market. They spread leaves down the center of the table like a runner, and set up candlesticks with tapers along with a few of the pillar candles.

Wendy stands with hands clasped. "Oh my goodness! This is amazing! Who would have thought . . . ?"

"Yeah . . . not bad," says Angela, putting her hands on her hips, pretty pleased with herself as she looks around the room. They then set the table and put the chairs in place.

As the tenants trickle into the dining room later that evening, there are muted oohs and aahs when they see the beautifully laid table. Many are not prepared for Thanksgiving dinner to be so much more of an event than just a basic turkey meal. Angela greets everyone as they enter. Jack is the last to come to dinner and peers into the room from the doorway, amazed at the transformation.

"Well . . . you certainly do know how to dress a room. It's beautiful." He places his arm around Angela's shoulders as if he has done it a hundred times before—and, incredibly, Angela does not feel a sudden urge to recoil. She actually surprises herself by leaning into him a bit. His arm around her shoulders feels natural. She hasn't felt so comfortable with someone— other than Jon—in so long. She breathes a sigh of relief not just for a job well done in dressing the dining room but also in feeling relaxed with people, a person, again.

The residents take seats along the side of the table and chatter excitedly to each other with a lot of smiles and laughter. Bob never joins the tenants in the dining room, but when he stops by the dining room to check on dinner—as is his normal routine—Angela takes him by the arm and leads him to the empty chair at the head of the table. He looks embarrassed and uncomfortable as he sits down, but Jack pats him on the back as he walks by and Bob relaxes and sets himself to enjoy a meal in his own dining room.

Wendy bursts through the kitchen doors with huge steaming bowls brimming with traditional Thanksgiving goodies. Mashed potatoes swimming in butter, sweet potatoes dripping in brown sugar, green beans with mushrooms, creamed onions, cornbread stuffing, cranberry sauce, relish trays, breads and rolls, and boats of gravy keep coming out of the kitchen. Then something amazing happens, when Cook herself waddles out of the kitchen bearing the antique ceramic platter burgeoning with a huge, beautiful, glistening, perfectly browned turkey on it. The group instinctively bursts into applause and Cook actually smiles. "How you say . . .

der ist more ver dat come from?" she says in her broken Germanic English. And everyone at the table laughs.

Cook places the magnificent turkey in front of Bob and turns back toward the kitchen, but Jack jumps up and ushers her to the chair at the opposite end of the table. "Today, we are one big happy family," he says as he pulls out the chair for her. Angela has reserved a seat for Wendy next to her and she starts passing bowls around the table. Then, when everyone is convinced they can eat no more, Wendy goes into the kitchen and starts bringing out the pies. Oh, the pies! Pumpkin pie decorated with tiny pastry leaves and sugared cranberries, apple crumble—heavy on the crumble and cinnamon, blueberry pie with a pierced sugar crust, and pecan pie with fresh whipped cream. The crusts are flaky, melt-in-your-mouth pastry and the fruit fillings perfectly balanced between tart and sweet with flawlessly balanced spices.

The joy and community in the room are palpable. Angela and Wendy have created a beautiful setting, Cook has delivered an amazing meal, and everyone thoroughly enjoys a true holiday—the first in years for many. Jack revels in this atmosphere, keeping the conversation going, telling jokes and stories, making sure everyone is engaged and entertained. It's a glorious Thanksgiving at Beauregard—a throwback to the time, so far in the past, when the house was a true family home.

CHAPTER 12

The weeks between Thanksgiving and Christmas are a bustle of activity. Angela's flair for party planning has reawakened and she has discovered her ingenuity in doing so on a tight budget. The success of Thanksgiving has made her especially excited about Christmas.

Jack is amazed at how Angela has blossomed. Nor does it go unnoticed by other people in the house. As Angela relaxes and opens up, so do the other tenants. The house seems a bustle of activity now with people in all the public rooms doing various activities and socializing. This is the house that Bob's aunt had envisioned—a house of community, friendship, and family for people that had none—and Bob is pleased that it has finally become just that.

With Bob's blessing, Angela sets about Christmas holiday decorating. Several nurseries from outside the neighborhood set up shop in parking lots around the neighborhood to sell trees. Angela and Wendy make the rounds a couple of times to pick up bits and pieces of branch trimmings and tie them with red plaid ribbon to make garlands to decorate the mantles, windowsills, staircase banister, and other places around the house. They have found boxes of glass ornaments and placed some in silver bowls on accent tables on top of some of the gold-trimmed linens which brighten up the library and sitting rooms. Already the house looks festive!

But something is missing.

Jack hasn't been around the house during the day much for a couple of weeks, but Angela assumes he is working. They meet for dinner every evening, and she is so excited talking about her day she forgets to ask about his. One afternoon, she's putting final touches to the mantle in the sitting room and chatting with Paulina and Herman when they hear a knock on the door. They look at each other—there is never a knock on the door. People just walk in. Herman looks out of the window. "Oh my goodness!" He jumps over to the door—and there is Jack with the biggest Christmas tree he's been able to find that will fit in the room.

"Thank you, sir. I couldn't manage the door and tree at the same time." He wrestles the tree into the sitting room and plops it in front of the window. "This will brighten up the place with some lights. What do you think?"

Angela is stunned. This is a big, fat, tall, beautiful tree. Lush and healthy and green . . . not like the sad little trees she sees around town. And already in a stand, ready for water. Normally, she would have been suspicious and wondered where he got such a fine tree. But today it doesn't matter. "Oh, Jack! It's perfect! Just what we need!" She throws her arms around his neck, hugging him tightly and kissing him on the cheek.

"Just wouldn't be Christmas without a tree. It's yours to do your magic." She knows from his smile how much her outburst of affection has touched him.

Angela brings up boxes of ornaments from the basement and readies everything for an old-fashioned tree-trimming event.

Cook makes hot cider and eggnog and delicate buttery cookies. Wendy pulls together the other residents to come and help—or at least socialize and have some treats. Henry has found some old records of Christmas music that he loads onto the ancient turntable. Stella and Louise seem to revert to their childhood, in awe of the wonderful tree and checking for Angela's approval for every ornament they place on it. Even Bob goes so far as to stand in the doorway, grinning at the good time everyone is having.

There are still a few days till Christmas Day, but everyone in the house can feel the holiday mood. It's as though no one has a care. For a few days at least, all their troubles have disappeared. But there's a snag. Angela has forgotten that Cook takes a couple of days at Christmas to visit her sister in the city. In the past, she has left plates of cold cuts, breads, and various salads and Wendy has laid them out. That just won't do this Christmas. This year it has to be special. This year has to be *perfect.* Angela would never ask Cook to cancel or even delay her visit, but she knows she doesn't have the skills it takes to handle a huge holiday dinner for this many people.

It is at dinner that Jack notices Angela seems worried. He places a hand on hers—something he does more often now. "Is something wrong?"

"It's Christmas dinner. Everything has been so perfect and I can't imagine having our usual deli trays for Christmas Day. You see, Cook leaves for a few days to visit her sister, and—"

"Say no more! Consider it dealt with!"

"What do you mean? What is dealt with?"

"I'll take care of everything. You've done so much. Now it's time for you to relax and enjoy. It's my turn now. Trust me. I know just what to do."

And she does trust him, though if she'd been asked why she could not have answered. She doesn't ask him again what he intends, and he doesn't say.

On Christmas Eve, there is more hot cider, more eggnog, and Cook has left them with quite an array of treats. A selection of savory mini pies—chicken with gravy pie, spinach and mushroom quiche, tomato pie, Swiss cheese and onion quiche—are baked to perfection. There is a loaf of potato bread filled with cheese and rosemary, asparagus puffs, German potato salad, cucumber salad, and dumplings swimming in a mushroom gravy. More melt-in-your-mouth cookies, tiny tarts with sugared berries on top, puff pastries, and small scones appear on the sideboard in the dining room. There isn't a single Scrooge in the house. Every single resident calls it the most incredible Christmas Eve feast they have ever enjoyed. They linger in the dining room, eating and chatting, long after they would usually have retreated to their rooms.

*   *   *

On Christmas morning, Angela wakes early. She pulls a robe over her pajamas and tiptoes downstairs, which is something she never did. Be seen in night garments? She figures it is early enough and she's desperate for a cup of tea—quite apart from being curious and just a little anxious to know what this plan is that Jack has hatched for today's dinner. She creeps down the stairs, avoiding the creaky steps, and floats toward the dining room. As she draws closer, she hears noise in the kitchen. Wendy must have beaten her to the tea. She pokes her head in and finds half a dozen people in white shirts, black trousers, and ties, with white aprons, all bustling about Cook's kitchen! One is sliding huge roasts of meat into the oven, another is peeling potatoes, while another chops green beans, onions, and carrots. People are pulling dishes from the cupboards and placing them on Cook's enormous center island. Angela is horrified. "Who are you and what are you doing here?"

And at exactly that point, Jack flies into the room. "This is my holiday surprise! We're having a big roast dinner!"

Angela is still confused. She needs that tea even more now. "Does Cook know about this?"

"Oh, yes. I cleared it with her days ago when I booked the caterers. She said as long as I made sure everything was cleaned up and put back, it was fine."

Her heart melts. Jack has to be the most thoughtful and considerate man she has ever met. And he thinks of everything.

One of the catering staff carefully places the serving bowl he is carrying on the counter and approaches Angela. "Would Madam care for some tea?"

She lets out a sigh of relief. Jack has taken charge, just as he said he would. She relaxes. "That would be lovely," she breathes. As she takes the steaming cup, she says, "Jack, this is amazing." Then she realizes that she is still in her robe. "But I really must get dressed." And off she goes, scurrying toward her room, her mind a mix of confusion about the wrongness of letting any man other than her husband see her in a state of even partial undress and just the slightest hint of excitement that it has happened. And that's just one more reason to be thankful that Jack is in her life—she can't imagine him making an improper move against a lady. He is a walking personification of decency.

*   *   *

Breakfast this Christmas morning is provided by the caterers. They lay out on the buffet a spread of pastries, scones, breads, rolls with an assortment of jams and jellies, and bagels with several varieties of cream cheese with lox and capers. On a gleaming silver tray are pitchers of freshly squeezed orange juice, along with a huge bowl of fresh fruit salad. The sun shines brightly through the windows as the residents file into the dining room. Just as on Thanksgiving, there are oohs and aahs as everyone studies the buffet and makes their selections. Even Wendy is not allowed to serve that morning, and she and Bob share a table for breakfast.

Everyone seems just that little bit more chipper this morning. They have pulled out their finest attire—a special brooch, a dapper jacket, a colorful sweater, or a vibrant scarf. And everyone is smiling and vibrant, their general misfit status forgotten as they come together as a family of their own making. Or of Bob's making, of course.

Angela returns in a mid-length black and red plaid skirt with a smart red sweater, black tights, and black flats, her hair pulled back loosely behind her ears. It's been years since she dressed for the holiday and today she feels good about the whole world. Jack is waiting for her at the doorway and she reaches out and takes his hand as they enter the dining room. "Oh, Jack—this is just lovely. How did you manage it?"

"Ohhhh . . . I sold a project and wanted to share my good fortune." He kisses her lightly on the cheek. "Merry Christmas, my angel."

Angela blushes and leans into his shoulder, totally absorbed in his affection and generosity and in this glorious morning.

The dining room is filled with the joyous sound of chatter and laughter and holiday cheer.

*   *   *

As people finish their meals, they retire to the sitting room to chat and admire the decorations and tree. The waitstaff stay on top of clearing dishes, keeping the dining room clean and tidy and avoiding disturbing the decorations. Eventually, everyone is gathered in the sitting room, chatting over cups of hot cider. In the background, holiday music plays on the old radio and Henry pulls out some old board games he found in a cupboard in the library, hoping someone might be interested in a game.

A familiar Christmas song comes on the radio and Jack startles everyone in the room when he bursts into song. The amazement is compounded when Henry joins in with an unexpectedly beautiful baritone voice. When the listeners clap and beg for more, a blushing Henry agrees, but only if everyone joins in. Soon the room is filled with the sound of the impromptu choir blending vigorous voices with some very frail and wavering ones.

Sitting enjoying the best holiday she can remember, Angela feels a gentle hand on her shoulder and turns to see Bob. He says, "You have a phone call."

Who would call her on Christmas Day? She can't imagine. She goes to the front desk and pics up the phone with some nervousness. "Hello?"

"Hey, Ange! How about I come over and pick you up and we'll find some holiday cheer!"

"Oh, Jon—how lovely of you to call!"

"Heather decided at the last minute to go skiing, and Robert is at the big house. Would you like to grab some dinner somewhere with me?"

"Oh, Jon, I can't tell you what a lovely day we are having here. Why don't you join your brother and his family ... at least for dinner? Or ... I'm sure there will be enough if you'd like to have dinner here?"

"Dinner *there?* You've NEVER invited me for dinner!"

"Well, this year is different. A Christmas angel has gifted us what looks to be the most wonderful roast dinner with all the trimmings."

"Wow, Ange—that sounds amazing! Enjoy your dinner! Can we get together this week?"

"Absolutely. I can't wait to see you."

"All right—let's catch up on Tuesday. I love you!"

"Love you too, my darling. Have a good day and don't be too hard on Robert."

"UGH. Okay. But just for you. See you Tuesday. Bye!"

CHAPTER 13

All afternoon, Wendy keeps jumping up from her chair in the sitting room to peek into the dining room. Finally, Jack goes with her and assures her all is under control. She says, "There's just never been anyone in Cook's kitchen except for Cook. She rarely even lets me do anything in there."

"I'm sure all will be fine. They wouldn't be in there without her prior approval." And a few minutes after Wendy has settled once more into a big overstuffed upholstered chair next to the simmering fire, one of the waitstaff comes to the doorway to announce that dinner is served.

The smell of a wonderful roast dinner fills the air as they move down the hall to the dining room where they are met by a fine spread of roast beef, turkey, roast potatoes, gravy, roast carrots, and cauliflower with a delicate cheese sauce. There is also a selection of breads and rolls, and piping hot Yorkshire puddings. Angela notices cranberries and chestnuts arranged around the roast meats, a nice festive touch, as well as appropriate sides including horseradish sauce, mustard, and cranberry sauce. Dinner is served buffet style, the meats hand-carved to each resident's order as they approach the table.

The individual dining tables are dressed with the normal white linens, but each table is decorated with greens with red berries and a candle. Lit candles line the buffet table and the windowsills. The lights have been lowered a little to allow the candlelight to fill the room for a magical effect.

Angela is meager in her choices, but realizes after the first couple of mouthfuls she probably could enjoy more of this mouthwatering meal. The roast beef and turkey literally melt in her mouth and the potatoes and vegetables are roasted to perfection. It rivals anything Cook would have produced.

Then comes dessert. The waitstaff lay out bowls of rice pudding and apple crumble with fresh whipped cream, poached pears with a berry sauce, and trays of Christmas cookies. Pots of hot coffee and tea are accompanied by more hot cider and eggnog with a dash of nutmeg. And, to cap a wonderful day, it turns into a white Christmas. No one has noticed that it has started to snow outside until they rise from their tables to head back to the sitting room, and they are drawn to windows to watch the snow glistening with the glow of candlelight.

Perhaps it's the day itself. Perhaps it's the beauty of the candlelight reflected in the snow. Perhaps it's something else entirely. Whatever it is, Angela feels moved to hold Jack back from the rest of the group as they filter out of the dining room. For a moment, they are alone. She takes his hand and moves close to him. He draws her into an embrace and kisses her tenderly. And she kisses him back. This is the most wonderful holiday she has had in a very long time.

*   *   *

In the following days, everyone in the house feels content and full of holiday cheer. There's a feeling of family in the house. Instead of retreating to their rooms, they linger in the sitting room and even the library filled with ancient volumes. Conversation and laughter can be heard throughout the house. Even Bob, a man of very few words who has always separated himself from the tenants, joins in. After the excitement of the holiday celebrations, life at Beauregard settles down to a comfortable pace. Jack is avoiding the coffee shop so his work slows, but it doesn't seem to be a hardship. The local bookstore has Wi-Fi and there's no filled-cup policy to be able to stay and work. Besides, the overstuffed upholstered chairs are far more comfortable than the straight-back wood chairs. Angela enjoys the bookstore and has found quite a few marketing resources to study there. She is glad to find a place to study within walking distance rather than having to slog through the snow and slush to the bus and then to the library.

They settle into a pleasant routine. First, breakfast in the morning to plan their day. Sometimes Angela has a commitment with Heather; other days she goes with Jack to wherever he plans to work. He makes a point of taking weekends off, and she is happy to do the same. A museum, a local art show, or just relaxing in the sitting room reading or playing chess make for relaxing weekend days. Then in the evening they enjoy dinner together and, if they've been apart, Angela tells Jack about her day. Jack never really mentions *his* work, and she assumes he is working on more inventions.

*   *   *

As a thank-you for his donation to the symphony orchestra, Jack has been gifted tickets to another concert. Angela is thrilled to accompany him—she has really missed cultural events, not to mention the opportunity to dig into the back of her closet and pull out some magnificent piece of eveningwear to enjoy.

Jack has hired a car for the evening since the roads and sidewalks are slushy. Just as they are about to leave, Jack's phone rings. He looks at the phone frowning, not recognizing the number, but when he listens to the call, Angela becomes alarmed for him when she sees the panic in his face. "What is wrong?"

He says, "There's been an accident . . . Remember that relative I came to find? I have to get to the hospital . . . Angela— I'm so sorry."

"Don't be. You must go! We can go to another concert. Don't worry!"

Jack runs down the walk and jumps into the hired car which speeds away. Angela watches it go, disappointed but understanding the urgency. Jack has never told her anything about this relative but she can only hope that whoever it is will be all right. It's odd, though—all the time they've spent together and he never even told her he'd found this long-lost relative. Who is it? She doesn't know. Well, she knows that side of Jack exists. Things he isn't ready to share. When she thinks about it, there's an awful lot she doesn't know about him. His past, what he's always working on . . . where he gets his money.

She climbs the staircase to her room, pondering the mystery that is still Jack. But, for all the things she doesn't know, there is one thing she is sure of. He genuinely cares for her. And that is enough for her, for now.

*   *   *

The car screeches to a halt at the emergency room entrance and Jack jumps out and runs in the door, almost colliding with a couple of wheelchairs parked nearby. He recovers himself and stumbles through the automatic doors. This is the most dismal emergency room he can imagine. Rows of seats in the waiting area are packed with the sick and injured. Some are filling out papers on clipboards, some are crying, some look vacant, staring into space as if drained of any hope. Some people hold towels or bandages against some body part, now red with blood. Some people sleeping across a couple of chairs look like they have been waiting for quite some time. A couple of teenagers lean against a wall, hunched over, peering at their phones.

The flickering lighting is oddly dim, as if the ceiling tube lights are all about to burn out, giving a creepy glow. The tile floors are worn and scratched and the pea-green walls add to the ghoulish effect. Beyond the desk he sees rows of partitions separated by curtains and wonders if Kara is in one of those. Alone and possibly frightened. The image of her as a little girl flashes through his mind.

It feels like he has stepped into a nightmare. At first repulsed, he starts to analyze how he could make this a better place. How he could *fix* this.

He tries to work his way through the crowds of people to the admissions desk, trying to get the attention of one of the nurses who look exhausted and frustrated. When he finally gets there, a nurse says, "Sir, you don't look in need of immediate medical attention. Please step away from the counter so we can assist those who need help."

"I'm here to see someone . . . to get someone. I . . . I got a call from someone that was admitted . . ."

"Name?"

"Jack Ford."

"That's the patient's name?"

"OH . . . no, no, that's my name. The patient is Kara . . ." Try as he does, he can't remember her mother's last name. "She was in a car accident. With her boyfriend. She just called me."

"Your relation to the patient?"

"I'm . . . I'm . . . her *father*." The words feel strange in his mouth.

The nurse flips through several clipboards of charts and papers and finally rests on a page. "Your daughter is a little banged up, but you'll be glad to know that she and the baby will both be fine."

"B, b . . . baby? BABY?"

She raises her arm over the crowded desk and motions to another nurse to take him to Kara's room. Jack follows the nurse down a hall from the emergency desk. The nurse points to a door. "In there." And then she's gone, hurrying back to the front desk.

Jack takes a deep breath and lets it out. He lays his hand on the door handle and is almost terrified to open the door. It's been weeks since he last saw her and she all but threw him out of the coffee shop. He doesn't want to upset her again, especially if she's going to have a baby. His grandchild! But she did, after all, call him. He pushes the door open a crack and peeks in.

Kara is asleep. This is the most calm he has ever seen her. Lying on her back and propped up by several pillows, her face and arms are covered in bruises and scratches. She has butterfly bandages on the right side of her forehead. Her left arm is hooked up to an IV. The dark circles under her eyes are even more pronounced, and her hair is a tangled, matted mess. She looks so serene. He slips into the room, sits in a chair positioned toward the end of the bed, and settles in to quietly wait.

A few minutes later, a nurse appears and, without saying a word, touches Kara's wrist and checks her pulse. Then she's gone as quickly as she came in, but the intrusion has roused Kara who blinks her eyes open. She seems disoriented. She looks round the room and a flash of panic passes over her face. Then she sees Jack at the far end of the bed. "I wasn't sure you'd come. I didn't know who else to call." It comes out as a hoarse whisper.

"Of course I came. You're my daughter. You did the right thing, calling me. Everything will be fine. Can I . . . ?" he says as he starts to stand with his hands on the arms of the chair.

She motions with her free hand for him to move closer. "Yeah, yeah. I don't feel like yelling across the room. Makes my head hurt."

Jack pulls the chair next to her. He feels so awkward, a new and foreign feeling for someone always so confident and organized.

"How bad is it?" Kara wheezes.

"They said you'll be fine. Banged up pretty good, but fine. Would you like some water?" Without waiting, he pours some from a plastic pitcher into a plastic cup and hands it to her. "And they said the baby is fine."

"Oh . . . yeah . . . about that. I'm pregnant. How about that? Two for one, right?"

"I couldn't be happier."

That gets him a smile. A weak smile, but a smile all the same. "I'm glad someone is happy about it."

"We'll figure it out." He pats her hand. "Uh . . . where is . . . ?"

"Joe? Oh. Well. Apparently the driver's side was totally crushed in the accident. And I saw them covering his face when they loaded me into the ambulance. He probably didn't feel a thing, he was so drunk."

Can she really be so calm when she tells him that? Or is she still in shock? Well, of course she is. "Oh no. Kara, I'm so sorry."

"Why? I'm not. I know that sounds harsh, but he was bad news and I just didn't have a way out. I never should have gotten involved with him. Story of my life. I always pick the wrong men. I don't know what's wrong with me." And then she starts to cry. "This is stupid! I don't cry!"

"You cry as long as you like. Just let it all out."

Tears stream down her face. She looks such a little girl, all Jack wants is to scoop her up and make everything right. He thinks about all the missed years, all the tears he couldn't wipe away, all the scraped knees he couldn't kiss and make better, and the bad breakups he couldn't soften with a hug and encouraging words. He has so much he needs to learn about this daughter he didn't until recently even know he had.

Kara struggles to pull herself up and Jack puts out his hands to steady her. She falls into his arms, sobbing. He holds her for what seems like hours until she falls back to sleep. He gently guides her back onto the pillows and sits back in the chair. This was not how he had wanted to connect with her, but he is glad the contract is finally made. He feels relief that she seems at last to accept him as her father. And not just her father, but someone she can count on.

And he's going to be a grandfather!

He watches her sleep, his mind already spinning with all the things he will tell her, all the things he will do for her . .

. and for his grandchild. Starting with the fact that he plans to open a branch office of his company in the area so that he can be near them both. And not just near to them, he reminds himself. That he is looking for a place to live—ideally to provide space for an extended family where a young child can have space to roam and to grow. Yes, as soon as he can, he'll tell Kara those things.

It's time, too, that he tells Angela. He is well aware of his habit of compartmentalizing things. He should be—it's got him into enough trouble over the years. He needs to bring Angela into his confidence. And as he has the thought, he realizes what holds him back. What if she says, "Your plans have nothing to do with me. Why are you telling me about them? Go and live wherever you want to—I don't care. If you think I have an interest in how you live your life and who you live it with, you delude yourself."

He convinces himself that perhaps the ground he stands on with Angela needs to be a little more solid before he opens up to her about what he intends to do. There's no hurry—she isn't about to leave Beauregard. She will still be there.

CHAPTER 14

Angela doesn't sleep at all the night before the engagement party. She is nervous not only because the wedding is the first big event she has helped plan in years, but because returning to Blythewood is daunting. She has not been back since her elder stepson, Robert, turned her out. She knows the family will be there and family friends she hasn't seen in years. Friends who disappeared after her husband died. She has never heard from a single one of them.

As the sun peeks through the curtains of her room, she sits and breathes a sigh of resignation. Her brain is racing with thoughts of all the people she might see, what they will think, how she will explain why the house is no longer hers. Slipping out of bed, she pulls on her robe and goes to the window to look out at the yard below. It's quiet, except for the occasional squirrel running across the lawn.

She sits at her dressing table, contemplating what to do. It's much too early to dress and she has no appetite for breakfast. She breathes deeply for a few minutes to calm her nerves. There's a knock on her door. Who on earth would be disrupting her on this of all mornings? She approaches the door with caution.

"Miss Angela? It's Wendy. I thought you might like breakfast in your room this morning?"

Angela smiles in relief and opens the door. "Oh, Wendy. You *are* thoughtful."

"I didn't expect you would want to bother with dressing for breakfast and then having to change for your party."

On the silver tray are a pot of hot tea, a cup and saucer, a pitcher of milk and a bowl of sugar cubes together with toast, a small plate with butter pats, and a bowl of strawberry preserves. A crisp white linen napkin is rolled into a silver napkin holder, and the utensils are polished and shining. A tiny vase holds a couple of sprigs of laurel, just starting to bloom.

"Oh, Wendy—this is lovely! How perfect."

"Take your time. If you think you'll want more tea, I'll be happy to bring it once I get the dining room set. Otherwise, I'll just collect the tray when you've gone so you're not bothered."

"This is wonderful—just enough. Thank you, Wendy." She places a hand gently on Wendy's shoulder. Two stepsons, but Angela has never had a daughter, and now presumably never will. Sometimes, her affection for Wendy makes her wonder how it would have been if she'd been blessed with one. She pours a steaming cup of tea and adds milk. She sips the tea as she wanders to the closet and pulls out the garment bag containing her dress. Pale blue chiffon with floral lace overlay, the tea-length, A-line dress looks perfect. The long sleeves end with three matching satin buttons at each wrist, and a row of the same buttons runs along the hidden zipper and trails down the back. Matching kitten heel shoes, small soft leather bag with silver buckle and strap, and the softly draping matching Japanese crepe coat complete the outfit.

It's been years since she wore this ensemble, but the look is timeless. Even the cleaner remarked how beautiful the dress was and marveled at the workmanship and detail. He took great care in cleaning the dress and coat and they look as new as they did the day she saw them on a fashion runway, decades earlier.

She turns on the radio and listens to some soft classical music while she finishes her tea and toast. She takes time over her shower and carefully blow-dries her hair so as to not let it frizz. She brushes it to a gleaming shine, the silver streaks glistening in the sunlight streaming through the window. She sweeps up her hair into a loose bun at the crown of her head, allowing curly tendrils to fall softly around her face and down her neck. She applies her makeup with a light hand, choosing pale rose shades that make her face glow.

She slips into her most glamorous silk lingerie and shimmering silk stockings. She carefully pulls open the garment bag and lifts out the dress, unzips the back, and steps carefully into it. As she pulls it to her shoulders and inserts her arms, it goes on effortlessly and fits perfectly.

From her jewelry drawer she takes white gold, diamond, and pearl drop earrings and a matching bracelet. She slips on her shoes and stands in front of the full-length mirror. Angela is not given to self-admiration, but she looks as though she has taken twenty years off her age. Then it's time for the crepe coat, after which she puts a few items in the handbag. She stands in front of her door and lets out a long, deep sigh before she opens it.

She walks along the hall and down the staircase and sees Jack waiting at the bottom of the stairs. He says, "Missed you at breakfast this morning. You look . . . amazing. Just amazing."

She blushes. What she is thinking is, "What about you?" Where did he get that beautiful worsted wool dark navy suit? What part of his life that she still knows too little about caused him to buy such a thing? A crisp white shirt with the palest blue pinstripe sets off his classic striped tie. He is so polished and dignified. And when did he get a haircut? His shoes are polished and—is it possible? Has he had a manicure? He looks an entirely different man.

He says, "I took the liberty of hiring a car for the day. Can't take the bus to a shindig like this." He puts out his hand and she takes it as they go down the front steps to a long, gleaming black car waiting at the curb. The driver jumps out and opens the back passenger car door, and Angela slides in easily. It's been so long—and yet she feels she belongs. Jack gets into the car from the other side.

On the drive to the party, Jack entertains Angela with animated small talk, something he is exceedingly good at. Angela soaks up his attention, the comfortable ride, and the beautiful day. When they reach the estate's front gate, the gatekeeper asks to see their invitation. Then they pass through the gate and drive up the long, gravel drive to Blythewood. Angela's breath catches in her throat. And Jack is aware of it. "Are you okay? We don't have to go in if you don't want to . . ."

"I'm fine. I just . . . It's so long since I've been here."

The trees seem taller and the landscaping more mature, but the house and grounds haven't changed. She suspects that is less because Robert Jr. wants to preserve the estate and more because he lacks interest in taking the time to do anything with it.

The car pulls up to the mansion's front steps and a staff member standing at the bottom of the stairs approaches the car and opens the back door for Angela. She exits the car looking up at the structure that had once been her pride and joy and a flood of emotions washes over her.

Jack comes round the back of the car and joins her, touching her elbow. Surprising herself, she slides her arm under his and they walk up the steps to the portico together. She walks tall and confident, part of her feeling like a queen returning to her castle, though it is her castle no longer.

They walk into the palatial two-story entry. There's a large circular inlay foyer table, with ornate legs and carving. On the glass tabletop is a huge arrangement of fresh flowers in a Chinese porcelain vase. Even though the traditional black and white tile floor gleams, Angela scrunches her nose disapprovingly when she sees dust on the enormous crystal chandelier hanging above the table.

The house buzzes with activity. White-gloved staff in white shirts and black trousers bustle around serving guests champagne and a wide selection of hors d'oeuvres from silver trays. There is chatter and laughter from the many people already here. Angela scans the room and sees a few familiar faces, but to her relief most of the people are new to her. They must be Heather's friends and family whom she has never met.

Moving toward the drawing room, Angela glances into the library across the hall. The massive wood-paneled room with thousands of volumes appears intact. Her late husband's enormous desk is still planted in the middle of the room facing the doorway, with two oversized leather wing-back chairs facing it. To the right is the fireplace with its custom carved marble mantle and surround. She catches her breath when she sees the painting over the fireplace. The portrait of her late husband and herself has been replaced with a portrait of him with his first wife. As she stares at it, she feels hands on her shoulders from behind. "I didn't know Robert had done that. I don't approve," Jon whispers. He is his casual self in gray dress slacks and loafers, with an open-collar white shirt with the sleeves turned up, his wavy blond hair already bleached by the sun.

"It's his house now. He can do as he likes."

Jon steps back to get a good look at Angela. "Wow, Ange. You look like a million bucks. Just—wow."

"You must be the lucky groom!" Jack booms as he brings two glasses of champagne, one of which he hands to Angela. "Hello, Jon. Glad to know you."

"And you must be Jack. I've heard so much about you— glad to finally meet." Jon puts out his hand to shake Jack's.

"Well," says Jack, "this is quite the place. A little dark, but . . . amazing."

"Perhaps Ange will give you a tour later. She knows this house better than anyone."

"You'd better get back to your bride-to-be," Angela murmurs. "Have fun and we'll catch up with you later."

"Okay, Ange. I want you to meet Heather's parents, so don't stray too far."

As Jon steps back, another young man approaches. He looks a bit like Jon, but is quite formal in a dark charcoal suit, starched white shirt, and black, white, and gray striped tie. He is taller than Jon and his dark hair is short and styled, a touch of gray starting to show at the temples. "Well, Angela. I see you were able to make it."

"Hello, Robert. Hope you and the family are well. The boys must be getting big. Robert, this is my friend Jack. Jack, this is Jon's older brother, Robert."

Jack thrusts his hand out to Robert. "Nice to meet you, Bob!"

"That's *Robert*. Thanks." He brushes off Jack's offer of his hand. "I'll—uh—catch up with you later." He turns and works his way into the crowded room.

To Angela, Jack's look of astonishment is only too obvious. Jon says, "Don't mind him. He's such a stuck-up. I don't know where he gets it. Look, you two have fun, there's tons of food and endless champagne. Please find me when you can so I can introduce you around." He hugs Angela tightly. "I'm so glad you're here. Jack? Take care of my girl."

Angela takes a deep breath and lets it out slowly. Well . . . that part is over. She had been dreading seeing Robert and the rest of the family. There are people everywhere, so Angela feels comfortable that no one will notice her taking Jack around the house. It's hard to see all the detail in the crowded drawing room, but from the doorway Angela points out the imported Persian rugs, the set of antique French armchairs of intricately carved mahogany upholstered in a burgundy textured jacquard fabric, and some other beautiful pieces. She notices that the carved mahogany Chippendale dining chairs have been moved into the room. There are several oversized armchairs, some with ottomans, all in a matching vintage burgundy, beige, and green floral print. The floor-length drapes are in the same fabric, and pulled to the sides of the windows revealing fine crocheted lace sheers. Dark wood wainscoting surrounds the room, and Angela points out that the burgundy wallcovering on the upper walls is actually silk rather than paper.

What she is thinking is that, when she originally designed this room, it was meant to be regal and bold. Now it just seems dated. She has an urge to buy gallons of soft-white paint and cover everything with it.

They slip out of the room and back into the hallway, where Angela describes the huge restorative project she had undertaken when she lived here. The plumbing and electrics were all updated, and she had insisted on preserving as many original fixtures as possible. The chandelier in the entry was once a candle-style chandelier and never used. She had it carefully wired and cleaned and now it is a showpiece on entering the house and almost always lit.

They work their way down the hall to get a glimpse of the kitchen, now buzzing with activity. She loves the white, raised panel cabinets and points to the long, marble-topped island with stools where Jon would sit to do his homework while Angela prepared an after-school snack or a light meal on the cook's night off. The original hand-painted delft tiles had all been removed, cleaned and repaired, and re-placed along the sides of the enormously long kitchen. The gleaming commercial-grade white tile had been installed to complement the blue delft tiles so they would "pop" against the white. She had installed high-end stainless steel appliances and wrought iron hanging racks dripped with copper pots and utensils. She made sure that the original Tudor style, hand-blown, leaded glass windows at the far end of the kitchen overlooking the backyard and lake were preserved.

They move through the people outside onto the terrace, Angela explaining how she had the brick exterior cleaned and broken bricks replaced with period materials and pointing out areas where the replacement bricks and mortar are practically invisible. They walk to the edge of the huge terrace and Jack is overwhelmed by the beauty of the grounds. Lilac bushes along either side of the terrace are starting to bloom and the air is filled with their subtle fragrance. On either side of the terrace are well-groomed gardens. To the right, the terrace gives way to a gravel path that leads through an English style garden boasting a beautiful array of flowers in various pastel shades, ornamental grasses, and decorative flowering trees, bordered on all sides by a trimmed hedge. At the far end, away from the house, is a weathered wooden bench, almost hidden from view by a pink rose-covered arbor. To the left of the terrace, accessible to the kitchen, is a cook's garden. A tiered platform closest to the house is filled with every imaginable herb and the rest of the garden consists of several raised beds of various vegetables.

The back end of the terrace is open to the expansive lawn sloping gradually downhill to the edge of a still lake. The late afternoon sun reflects in the calm water and there is a slight breeze. Jack hears the sounds of birds in the lush forest that surrounds the entire estate—it's almost as if he is standing in a private nature preserve. He realizes he has never lived in a place so serene, so well-cared for, and vows to himself to own a property like this. "This is just amazing. I see now why you were so sad to have to leave." He places a comforting hand on her arm.

Angela appreciates his comfort and turns away so he doesn't see her eyes welling with tears. "We should get back to the party." Then she says, "In fact, Jack, I'm not sure . . ."

"You're finding the emotional cost a little too high?"

"Do you mind?"

"Not at all. I'll call the car and we'll go back to Beauregard. Or maybe find some other entertainment. There's a park not far away—a walk through the woods? Buy a picnic and eat it by the lake?"

"Jack, that sounds wonderful. Thank you for being so understanding."

They make their way through the crowded drawing room heading toward the entry. She spots Jon talking with Heather and a group of her girlfriends just near the doorway of the drawing room, and he breaks away when he sees them. "Not leaving so soon, are you? I haven't even introduced you to Heather's family!"

Angela touches Jon's elbow and they step around the corner just outside the doorway. "Oh it's fine. I'll meet them at the wedding. It's been a bit emotional, coming back here today. You don't mind, do you? I'll see you next week, okay?"

"I'm so glad you came—I understand. I'm happy you could be here, even if just for a while. Let me walk you both out." He turns to Jack. "Thank you for bringing my Ange. I'm not sure she would have come at all if she didn't have . . ."

They have just stepped into the doorway when they overhear Heather's booming voice. "Jon suggested her and I said yes because she has nothing better to do and she would work cheap. Oh yes, she has good taste. But you would think she could open her tight purse strings a little to buy a new dress? That 'vintage' thing only goes so far. She's still wearing clothes from twenty years ago. Can you imagine?! And she can't run a little dye through her hair just for today? Hope she doesn't show up like that at the wedding. It will just *ruin* the pictures!"

The drone of the crowd instantly dims and the room goes quiet. All eyes are on Heather, whose bleached blonde hair bounces on her shoulders as she looks around the room, oblivious to the presence of Angela and Jon right behind her. At last, the silence and the stares cause her to swing around and see them. Her face turns bright red. "I . . . I thought they had left!"

Jon steps forward and takes Heather's elbow as if to lead her away, but she jerks out of his grasp. Jon turns his back to the people surrounding Heather, backs her toward the wall, and bends his head toward her ear. After a brief, tense, unheard discussion, he looks up and turns to face the crowded room.

"Thank you all for coming. I'm afraid this engagement party will NOT be followed by a wedding. This engagement is over. The wedding is OFF!" He storms out of the house.

CHAPTER 15

Angela decides this is not the time for a romantic lakeside picnic and walk through the woods. The ride home from Blythewood is pretty quiet. Angela is heartbroken for Jon and stares out the window the better part of the drive. Jack sits close to her in the back of the car, occasionally patting her hand. Finally, she just can't contain herself any longer. "Oh, Jack. What a tragedy. I feel like I'm the cause of this."

"Then stop. How could you be? She's probably been like that her whole life. It's nothing you did and there's nothing you *could* have done."

"If I weren't so gullible . . . I just wanted to do what she wanted, and now to find out she was just using me because I was inexpensive . . ."

"That's right! She was *using* you. I can't understand such shallowness. What difference does it matter what you wear? It's supposed to be a joyous family event!"

"Please don't get upset. It's over and done. I just feel so bad for Jon. He must be livid."

"Better to learn her true nature now than to marry her and find out just how snarky she and her friends are."

"I hadn't thought of it that way. It's true—we should be thankful. And Jon is a young man. He'll find someone more suitable. If she'd bothered to ask, I could have told her that I *did* splurge on a new outfit for the wedding to complement her colors . . . a dress that she actually suggested. Or, rather, vehemently encouraged."

"Then you know what you must do. Take it back. Exchange it for something amazing to wear for a special evening out with me! Let's celebrate Jon's freedom!"

"I WILL. I'll do it tomorrow."

"Wonderful. I have some things to do tomorrow, but let's plan a celebratory dinner."

That night, Angela slept deeply. The pressure of the wedding was off, she knew in her heart that Jon was better off and would bounce back, and Jack had helped her make sense of the broken engagement.

Jack, on the other hand, couldn't sleep at all. He was excited like a child on Christmas Eve. This was it. Tomorrow night he would reveal all to Angela . . . his daughter, his grandchild, his "real" story . . . and ask her to be his partner for life.

*   *   *

Jack is already gone when Angela arrives for breakfast, but there's a note on their table. "Pick you up at 6:00. It'll be a night you won't forget. –Jack"

Angela hasn't had a night she won't forget in a long time. Just what is he planning? She finishes breakfast and waltzes upstairs to pack up the dress she had bought for the wedding. Heather specifically requested that the bridal shop owner help Angela choose a dress that would "complement" the bride. At the time she purchased it, she thought it was a bit matronly, but after all she was the groom's stepmother. Looking at it now,

Angela finds the slim-fitting skirt of the silver, tea-length satin sheath dress not particularly flattering. In fact, it makes her look disproportionately "hippy." And the huge arrangement of matching fabric flowers cascading from the jewel neckline down the right front of the dress is more than a little garish with the extensive beading and lace incorporated into the arrangement. Overall, the dress is over the top. But then, so is Heather.

The dress still has the tags and is still in its bag. She bundles it up and hails a cab to the dress shop. She doesn't want to risk anything happening to it between here and the store, so best carry it by car.

The shop owner is understanding about the cancelled wedding, and refunds her money. "Too bad," she says. "This dress *totally* suited you!"

Angela thanks her and keeps her opinion of the dress to herself. As she stands outside the store deciding where to head next for a replacement dress, a large, polished black car pulls up in front of the baby store across the street. It looks familiar, but there must surely be more than one black car service in the area. She gives herself a moment of pleasure in the implied arrival of a new baby. And then her world turns to dust. A man jumps out of the car and tenderly helps a very pregnant Kara step out and up onto the curb. The man is Jack.

She stands for a few moments trying to make sense of what she is seeing. The pair of them are oblivious to her watching them from the opposite side of the street. Jack hops up to the door of the baby store and opens it, taking Kara's elbow and leading her through it to enter before him. His face is beaming. As you would expect in a man shortly to become a father.

She struggles to piece together what she has just seen. Is Kara the "long-lost relative" he came here to find? Or was that just some story he made up to shut down her questions? So THAT'S where he is when he's not with me. THAT'S why he's always hanging out at that coffee shop.

Ancient insecurities rise to the surface, feeding her anger not only at Jack but also with herself for being so trusting. So gullible. She has always known there was something off about Jack, something he hid, but she let herself get swept up in his generosity and good-natured treatment. How could she have so blindly trusted him? She should have followed her first instinct to steer clear of him, but he seemed so authentic, so genuinely caring, so kind. Furious, she catches the next bus to the house, fuming the entire ride. She retreats to her room, her emotions reeling.

CHAPTER 16

Jack returns to the house happy. He skips up the front steps and actually notices himself whistling as he enters the front door. Life is good. He has found his long-lost daughter and she, and his future grandchild, are now safe and comfortable. He had been looking for a permanent place to live and the perfect situation just opened up. His plans are falling into place. And in Angela he has found the partner he never dreamed he would have.

Until now, he hasn't wanted to cross the line with Angela. He knew the danger of overwhelming her too soon with why he was here and what he had found. He didn't want anything to spoil the pleasure he finds just being in her company. But now that Kara has accepted him, he can help her with a safe home, and there's a new baby on the way, and considering the strength and stability of his feelings for Angela, which he is pretty sure she reciprocates, he is confident he's gone about this the right way—and now he is ready to tell Angela everything. He bounds up the staircase and knocks on the door to her room to see if she's ready. There's a pause, and then behind the door he hears her move down the steps from her room to the door. She opens the door slowly and leans on the doorjamb, her arms folded across her body.

"Hello, beautiful! Let's get out of here for a while. How about a stroll to our favorite Italian spot?"

"I don't think so."

She's unhappy about something. "What's up?"

"Just what did you think you were doing?"

"Doing? About what?" He's done something to upset her, that's obvious. But what?

"I saw you today."

"Saw me . . . where?"

"At a baby-goods store."

"Did you?" He laughs. "That's part of what I want us to celebrate tonight."

"Really?"

"You see, when I came here . . ."

"You didn't think you'd meet someone like Kara. Is that what you wanted to tell me? My goodness, Jack. She's young enough to be your daughter."

"Well, as a matter of fact . . ."

"And all the time you were doing what you were doing with her you were leading me on! Didn't you think I'd find out eventually?"

"Well . . . I was keeping things separate. I think to keep things compartmentalized . . ."

"Compartmentalized? You put me in a box? To take out and play with from time to time, when the person you're really serious about isn't available." She's aware that she is close to screaming; even from up here, other residents must be able to hear what's going on. She doesn't care.

Jack says, "Can we talk about this calmly?"

"Talk about what? How you betrayed me? I've been betrayed before and I will NOT let you embarrass me any more than you already have. You've made me look like a fool. I don't want to see you ever again!"

"There's a perfectly logical explanation, but . . ." She slams the door in his face.

As he hovers outside the door to her room, he realizes he should have been straightforward with her from the start. It wouldn't be the first time someone has told him that his habit of keeping parts of his life in separate compartments would one day blow up on him. He'd wanted to protect Angela. He should have given her more credit. She's taken care of herself for this long, after all the rough spots she's been through. She didn't *need* protecting.

He returns to his room to write it all out—to explain everything—that Kara is actually his daughter with a grandchild on the way and to apologize for not trusting Angela or confiding in her. He'd intended to write a short note but the words just pour out and he finds himself writing several pages. He wants her to know everything. He wants to share everything with her.

He folds the sheets, slips them into an envelope, and seals it. He tiptoes to her room and slips the note under her door. And as soon as he's done it, he knows he should have done it differently. He should have left it for her at the desk so she'd have time to cool off before picking it up. Well, what's done is done. Just as his poor decision in withholding his plans from Angela for months is done. He realizes there is no recovering from what he has hidden from her. In a way, she's right. In a way, he really has betrayed her.

He goes back to his room and starts to pack. The plan had been to ask Angela over dinner to accompany him to his new home. He'd delayed his move to find the right time to invite her to go with him. A right time that he now realizes should have been much earlier. There seems to be no point staying longer than one more night, and all he can do is hope she will read his letter and forgive him by morning.

*   *   *

Angela is curled up on her bed. The tears rolling down her face are a mixture of anger and sadness. She can't believe he hid so much from her for so long. She can't believe she fell for him and let him lead her on. She should have stayed guarded and protected her heart. All the old grief and anger from the past are bubbling up. Her husband betrayed her by not providing for her—he had to have known his will had not been updated. How could he not? He continually told her it was in the works and he would do it. Was he lying to her all those years or did he really think it was handled? Did he never intend to leave her the estate that she had put her heart and soul into restoring and making a home? Was she just a means to an end for him, as she had been for Heather? Did she serve her function and what happened to her after he died didn't matter? His lack of a signature on the revised will told her all she needed to know, although she had ignored the clear message at the time.

She hears the letter slide under the door. She doesn't move. She is frozen with fury. All she wants is to go to sleep and forget everything. She pulls the covers over herself. The rest of the world can stay where it is on the other side of the door. She closes her eyes and gives in to the exhaustion of her anger.

*   *   *

Next morning, Jack opens the door to his room and sticks his head out, checking up and down the hall. He emerges from his room, setting out his bags and the boxes of things he has accumulated since his stay at the house as gently as possible. He doesn't want to disturb any of the other residents, and he certainly doesn't want another confrontation with Angela. He's hoping to leave discreetly and as silently as possible.

He carries his bags down the stairs, trying to avoid every groan and creak. He sets them down by the front door, and creeps back upstairs to bring down the boxes.

The front door opens with its characteristic creak, and Jack cringes. A black car waits at the end of the walk, and the driver jumps out to help Jack with his bags and boxes. Jack pats the man on the shoulder and retreats into the house to settle up with Bob, who waits for him at the front desk. "Thank you for everything," says Jack. "Thanks for your very kind hospitality."

"I'm sorry to see you go. You brought a little life to this tired old house."

Jack looks up from writing a check. "Well, I've done what I came to do and now it's time to leave. And . . . it's a grand house. I hope we'll meet again."

"What about Angela? Isn't there anything you can say or do?"

"Not right now. She's upset. She thinks she saw something she didn't see. She doesn't understand that I was spending time with the daughter I didn't know until recently I had—"

Bob's eyebrows rise in surprise. "You have a daughter? *Here?* Of all places . . ."

"That's why I came here. I found her and now I can take care of her. But I also found so much more . . . Well. Sometimes you eat the bear. And sometimes the bear eats you. I should have told Angela much earlier what was happening."

"You think it's too late?"

"I've based my whole life on the idea that it's never too late. I think I've been wrong this time."

"You're welcome to come by anytime. I can't say I can top that holiday feast we had, but I can certainly give you a good meal and some company."

"You're a good man, Bob. I'll miss you." He pats Bob on the shoulder and turns down the hall and out the front door. In the early morning stillness, Bob hears the car door close and the car pull away.

The house is silent, the clock's ticking the only thing audible. Bob stands motionless, soaking in the silence. It feels like the energy was sucked out of the house when Jack closed that door behind him.

*   *   *

Angela, too, has woken early, too tired and drained to sleep anymore. She hears Jack moving about the house and, when she hears the front door shut, peers from behind the lace curtains to watch him walk slowly to the car, climb into the back, and drive away. She stands for some time at the window, frozen. At last she turns from the window and moves toward a chair to sit down when she notices the envelope by the door. She picks it up hesitantly and holds it for a moment, turning it over and over in her hands, debating whether to open it or not. Why bother? It can only be some self-serving excuse. Had she heard anything from him but lies since the day he came to this house? That wasn't going to change now. He isn't worth any more of her time. She tears the letter into pieces and drops it in her wastebasket. She bursts into tears and falls into the chair.

CHAPTER 17

Angela has retreated to her room, unable to face the other tenants, or anyone. Not even Jon. When Wendy doesn't see her at meals for a second day, she puts a breakfast of hot tea and whole grain toast with butter and jam on a tray, creeps up the creaky stairs, and approaches the door to Angela's room. She knocks gently on the door. She hears shuffling behind the door and eventually Angela opens the door a crack. "Oh, Miss Angela. You need to eat. You have to eat something!"

"I just can't. I just want to be left alone for a while. I'm sorry you went to all this trouble." She starts to push the door closed.

"Wait! Let me just leave it and you see how you feel. Okay?"

"All right. Come in." She opens the door wide and Wendy slides into the room and sets the tray on a table. It is stuffy in the room. Angela needs fresh air.

"May I open a window? It's really a beautiful day and I think you might like some fresh air with your tea!"

"Oh . . . I suppose. If you like." She crumples back into a chair.

Wendy opens the window closest to the door so as to not tread too deeply into Angela's domain . . . Or her grief. "I'll come for your tray in a bit and check on you. Okay?"

Tears well in Angela's eyes. "Sure. I appreciate your care."
Wendy slips out the door and quietly pulls it closed behind
her. Angela sits in her chair for a few minutes, waking up to
the fresh air in the room. The scent of the tea and jam wafts
through the room and entices her to pour some tea. It tastes
amazing. She feels its warmth move down her throat into her
stomach and immediately feels more energized. She butters
and spreads jam on a slice of toast and takes a small bite. After
a couple more bites and the rest of the tea, she is full and leaves
the rest of the toast on the plate, curling up in the chair with a
fluffy throw and a book. She eventually dozes off.

After a couple of hours, Wendy returns for the tray, again
knocking gently at the door. Angela rouses herself and answers
the door, allowing Wendy into the room. "Oh wonderful! You
drank all the tea. Would you like some more?"

"Well . . . to be honest, it was quite tasty. Perhaps I . . ."

"I'll take this away and be right back." She is soon back
with more tea on a tray. As she pours a cup for Angela, she
talks about who had what for breakfast that morning, and
what she's been learning in her classes, and whatever else she
can think of to keep Angela distracted and engaged. Angela
tries to listen and realizes that Wendy is just trying to cheer
her up. Eventually, she tires of her chatter.

"Oh, Wendy, thank you for the lovely tea. I think I'd like to
have a little alone time now, if that's all right?"

"I'm so sorry! I've just been rambling on! I'll leave you to
it then."

"Thank you. I appreciate it."

As Wendy leaves the room, she turns. "How about I bring
you a little soup for dinner? Cook has made a wonderful
minestrone that looks amazing!"

"Well . . . we'll see. Check back later?"

"Absolutely!"

Angela dozes for a short time and debates whether it might be time to get herself together and clean up. That man has played havoc with her life. Is she going to let him turn her into a recluse? She pulls some comfortable clothes from the far reaches of her closet and lays them on the bed. She takes a long shower and washes her full, wavy hair, deliberately working the shampoo and conditioner through it. After finishing her shower, she dries and moisturizes her skin and face and dries and combs her hair. She dresses slowly and deliberately. She feels like she's recovering from an exhausting illness, and cleaning up and dressing make her tired all over again—but at least she is clean.

That evening before the dining room opens, Wendy returns, carrying a tray with a bowl of fragrant soup accompanied by some crusty bread and butter with a glass of ice water and lemon. She switches the tea tray with the dinner tray and tells Angela she'll be back later to collect it.

The soup smells amazing, and Angela tears off a small piece of bread and dips it into the steaming bowl. Heaven! It's so delicious. Angela eats all the soup and all the bread and feels very satisfied.

She curls back up in her chair to think. So what if Jack is a schmuck? Is she going to let him ruin her life? Over the last few months she's learned so much and discovered things about herself she didn't know . . . or had forgotten. Was she just remembering her old self? She should be grateful to Jack for bringing all that out of her—the gifts he gave her, both physical and intangible. He had coaxed her true nature and sense of self out of her.

She smiles as she thinks of the wonderful experiences she had with him. And she sees that they hadn't done anything she couldn't have done herself. And she should have. Why was she so upset? It isn't as if she had known him for decades, or lost him as she lost her husband. No promises had been spoken; no commitments made. Any obligations were never put into words. It was just a bit of fun, right? Nice while it lasted. Apparently, they had had different agendas.

Still, she can't help wondering why he had worked so hard to gain her trust, just to throw it away. That doesn't make sense.

Wendy taps on the door. "May I take your tray?"

"Oh certainly! Thank you for being so kind, Wendy. You are—and always have been—a good friend."

Wendy blushes. She looks at the empty dishes. "That soup must have been tasty!"

"It was brilliant. As usual. Please thank Cook for me."

"I will. Shall I bring your breakfast tomorrow morning?"

"No, Wendy. It's time I came out of hiding. I'll be down tomorrow morning, ready for the day."

She sees Wendy struggling not to dance a jig when she hears this. Honestly, has she put people to so much worry on her account? She should be ashamed. But all Wendy says as she backs out of the door with the tray is, "Sleep well."

Angela dresses for bed and slips under the soft, billowy covers. A gentle breeze from the slightly open window cools the room, making it ideally comfortable. Her body relaxes and she thinks about Jack. She misses him. She will probably go on missing him for a while yet. But she can live with that. What she needs to do—and she makes this promise to herself—is to take advantage of whatever opportunities come her way instead of trying to shoehorn herself back into an industry that has outpaced her. If Jack has taught her nothing else, he has taught her to be content and appreciate what immediately surrounds her. And there is so much that she has totally missed!

Perhaps the world holds something new for her. Something more interesting than her old life? She drifts off to sleep, actually looking forward to what tomorrow will bring.

*   *   *

Next morning, the sun shines brightly through the curtains in Angela's room. She wakes gently, slowly, and feels unexpectedly refreshed. The sense that there are opportunities everywhere has not disappeared in the night.

She dresses for the day, brushes through her hair, and starts to pull it back into her customary tight bun. But why? Why pull it back so tightly? She clips it loosely with a large barrette at the base of her neck. It feels more comfortable that way. She pulls on some flat shoes and a loose cardigan since the breeze coming in the window feels a bit cool. She walks quietly down the hall and creeps down the stairs. She is embarrassed by the public way things ended with Jack, and for hiding in her room, and suddenly cringes at the thought of painful looks from the other residents. And then she surprises herself. Never mind that, she thinks. Let anyone think what they like. We'll all get over it. She straightens herself up and steps confidently into the dining room. Everyone is present. For a moment she wishes she had come down early and been on her way out rather than walking into a room full of people.

She takes a deep breath and heads to her table at the far side of the room. As she passes each table on the way to hers, they all acknowledge her and greet her with smiles, nods, and greetings of "Good morning." All normal behavior. She had dreaded seeing pity in anyone's eyes. It isn't there. They are all family now, and what they want is to support her in doing whatever makes her happy and comfortable.

Wendy is thrilled that she has emerged for breakfast. "Miss Angela! How are you this lovely morning? What can I bring you?" she asks a little too loudly. Then, much more softly, she whispers, "I'm so happy to see you."

Angela smiles at her. "I'm okay. Everything is going to be okay." Loudly enough for everyone to hear she says, "I'll have the usual, please, Wendy."

"I'll have your tea right out."

Angela lets out a sigh of relief. She actually does feel that everything will be okay. She is a new person—or perhaps she has just found a part of her she had lost? She notices that the other tenants appear to be conversing across tables, sharing a paper or a story they recently heard. She hadn't noticed this before, probably because she was so focused on Jack during their meals. It is lovely that everyone is conversational and engaging. And that togetherness, that sense of community, is something she knows they owe to Jack. It came into existence at Thanksgiving and it was cemented at Christmas.

As she eats, Angela mulls over what she should do with the day. Back to job hunting no doubt. But let's be smart about this. She's learned some useful skills and there's no point wasting them. And it's a beautiful day. Perhaps a walk around town before the weather turns is more in order?

It comes to her that she has choices. She can *choose* how to spend her days. Her room and board are covered by her stipend, after all. She has good food and shelter. That's more than many people have, and she is thankful. Perhaps if she takes the pressure off herself and lets things unfold, the perfect opportunity will come. Maybe even in a way she least expects. Encouraged by this line of thinking, she is wrapped in a warm wave of gratitude she never really experienced before. She used to take things for granted. And she shouldn't. Because life is a gift ... HER life is a gift.

As she leaves the dining room, she passes by the front desk where Bob is sorting the mail.

"Good morning, Bob. I don't suppose there's anything for me?"

"Good morning, Angela. No—I didn't find anything as yet. But the mail is a bit sparse today. I'll let you know." She lingers for a moment, as if there is more to say. Bob pauses his mail sorting and looks up over his glasses. "Pretty quiet around here."

Angela looks down at the counter, drawing imaginary circles and figure eights on it with her finger. "Yes ... a bit." She looks up at Bob. "But it's okay," she says calmly and confidently, laying her hand flat on the counter.

Bob says, "I guess we'll never know if he found the person he was looking for. He mentioned something about having a daughter—"

"Well, she may have been young enough to be his daughter, but I think there was something else going on there ..." When Bob raises an eyebrow, she says, "I'm sorry. That wasn't nice at all, was it?"

"You have the right to feel what you feel. There just has to be more to why he was here. It wouldn't make sense otherwise."

Angela climbs the stairs to her room slowly and deliberately. Looking around, she feels a little lost, not sure what to do with herself. The idea that she could do whatever she pleases was a freeing revelation, but it also leaves her feeling disoriented. She stands in the middle of the room and looks around. It's about time for a good tidy. She decides that some of the chairs and tables need to be moved to something more efficient. Then she opens the canvas closets. She will most likely never wear many of these clothes again, so why not free herself of this burden? It's time to purge.

She pushes through the racks, pulling out clothes and tossing them onto the bed and chairs. She rummages through her drawers, making a pile in the middle of the floor. Didn't she see a clothing consignment shop in town? Perhaps they would be interested in some of her better suits and dresses. The rest she could donate.

She's on a roll. She goes through her shelves of books. She's read some of them multiple times. Perhaps it's time for someone else to get pleasure from these tired volumes. Then she starts on her jewelry, her hats, her scarves, gloves, and coats. So many memories, not all of them good. She keeps what is special and makes a separate pile of items that Wendy might like.

In her cleaning fury, she looks at the laptop sitting on a table. She feels a pang remembering how Jack taught her how to use it, set up an email address, and build her résumé. Is that, too, to go on the pile of books? No. She should use it. It was a gift from Jon after all. And she invested all that time learning to use it. It certainly would save on bus fare and hassle. She decides she will go to the bookstore the following day and use it.

CHAPTER 18

Next morning, Angela is drawn to do something she didn't think she would dare do—walk past the coffee shop. She doesn't expect to see Kara there, but she can't help being curious. And there's a "Help Wanted" sign in the window, so presumably Kara has left. Well, why wouldn't she? Jack isn't going to want his paramour working in a coffee shop. She's about to walk on when a thought pops into her head. Could she? Would she? DARE she? She peeks in the window and sees that Kara is there, after all. She is about to move on—but why should she? This is a job she could do in her sleep. And if she applies and gets it, Kara will be able to go on her way. And, face it—the chances of Jack returning to the shop are slim.

She takes a deep breath. How will she explain her total lack of experience? But then the killer question: What does she have to lose? What's the worst that can happen? She'll be turned down. Big deal. She pushes open the door and approaches the counter where Kara is speaking to a man behind it, while trying to clean up and fill the pastry cases. The morning rush is over and the place is in disarray.

Kara turns to look at her. "Well, it's YOU! Haven't you done enough damage? If you're looking for Jack, he isn't here."

"Why would I be looking for him? Clearly, he is not interested in me."

"Don't come the innocent with me. Jack Ford is the kindest man I've ever met in my life, and he loved you to distraction, and you ..."

"Kara. Please. Stop. I don't ... it's pretty hard to believe he really cared about me once you entered the picture ..."

Kara's face reflects stunned astonishment. "Are you serious? What were you thinking?! Jack is the best father ..."

"Well. I'm sure he will be."

The man behind the counter appears flustered by the two women's confrontation. "Kara, is there a problem here?"

"No. No problem that can't be fixed by one of us leaving." Kara throws a cloth across the room. "Why did you come in here, anyway? You always looked so superior when you came in with him."

"I came to apply for the job."

Kara turns to the man. "Well, Frank, this is—or WAS—one world-class hostess, party-planner, Miss High-and-mighty. I'm sure her hostess experience will really come in handy at your little coffee shop. Perhaps she'll drum up some magnificent marketing campaign for you while she's at it!"

Kara tosses her keys on the counter, spins around, and heads toward the back door, grabbing her jacket off a rack on her way out sending the rack crashing to the floor.

Stunned, Frank looks at Angela and after a few moments says, "When can you start?"

*   *   *

Following a few days of training and keeping the shop tidy and clean, the owner hands her the keys and she's on her own.

Her experience as a society hostess comes in handy, keeping the customers happy and cups filled. She comes to love the daily interaction, the chitchat, recognizing the regulars, and selling an extra baked good here and there. And it's nice to have a small income, though she finds the money matters less to her than having a purpose, somewhere to go most days. Her days now have new meaning. Not the meaning she'd originally envisioned, but she's useful and productive.

Sometimes she stays after closing and does a little job hunting with her laptop, although the urgency and panic have waned. All she wants is to keep her eyes on the listings in case the perfect opportunity shows itself. She has let go of the anxiety, but she can't shake the feeling that something else is out there. Something more. That the opportunity of a lifetime is just around the corner. All she needs is to stay open and alert.

*   *   *

After everything that has happened, Angela is anxious to reconnect with Jon. How is he bearing up? Is it still all over between him and Heather? He assures her it is. They plan dinner at his apartment. Just like old times.

He insists on sending a car, and this time she doesn't argue. It's actually a relief to have reliable transportation to and from his place. She's learning to accept Jon's kindnesses and not to be quite so stubborn.

When she rings the bell to his apartment, the door swings open. "Oh, Ange—it's so good to see you. I've missed you!" He hugs her so hard she feels she might break.

She pulls back and holds his face in her hands. "Oh, my love, I've missed you too. So much has happened."

They go to the kitchen where Jon is grilling salmon with asparagus and checks on the jasmine rice. He says, "You said on the phone Jack has left? What happened?"

"I made a complete idiot of myself. I'm sorry, Jon, I don't want to talk about it." She doesn't want to reveal all she had seen or anything about their argument.

"Surely something must have prompted him to go. You two really seemed to get on so well . . . are you sure there wasn't something that made him leave?"

"Well . . ." She takes a deep breath. "I saw him with the girl from the coffee shop at a baby store. And she was pregnant."

"Okay . . . And so?"

"Don't you see? He met her at the coffee shop and, well, you know." She shrugs.

"Do you really think what I think you're thinking?"

"He came to find someone, and he did. Then he left. End of story."

"He came to find someone . . . perhaps she was the one he came to find. Perhaps he didn't just 'meet' her, but he came to find her. Perhaps they were related somehow, and he knew she needed help . . ."

"Bob at the house mentioned that he had said something about a daughter . . ."

"That's it! Of course. She must be his daughter. That makes perfect sense!"

"Oh, Jon . . . I don't know."

"Didn't he explain? I'm sure he didn't just disappear without trying to explain. He didn't strike me as that sort of guy."

"Well . . . he did leave a very bulky note. But I couldn't read it. I tore it up."

"You WHAT?"

"I know, I know—it was stupid. I should have taken time to cool off."

"It wasn't stupid. It's totally understandable considering what you thought you saw. But I really don't think he was out to use you. Or use anyone. I think he genuinely cared for you."

She sighs. "Well, whatever the facts, it's over now. It's not like we made any commitments to each other. At least none that were spoken. It was nice while it lasted and I'm getting on with things. And what about you? How are you? I'm so sorry how things ended for you with Heather. I was so disappointed about the broken engagement."

"I was angry for a while. Then I realized she wasn't right for me. She was just after my name and my money—or what money she *thinks* there is. I don't think she knew that the money I get is just a fraction of Dad's estate and I don't have any claim to the house. When I called off the wedding, I did her the favor of helping her avoid a pretty average life."

"She was the teeniest bit over the top. She certainly had interesting taste." As soon as the words are out she regrets saying them.

But Jon is laughing. "Tell me what you really think, Ange!"

They settle down to eat and chat about mundane things. As they are finishing, Jon says, "Oh—and there's news about Blythewood. Robert has sold it."

"What? Who to?"

"Some businessman relocating to the area. A huge aeronautics engineering company bigwig. He said he was moving his headquarters to the city, but he wanted a home in the country. He said he had seen Blythewood at one time and he made Robert an offer."

So a stranger is going to live in the home she spent so much effort to restore and decorate. Well, perhaps she should be relieved that Robert will no longer be living there. Perhaps this unknown man will have a better appreciation for her restorative efforts than her stepson ever did. "Really?" she says. "That's amazing!"

"Yup. I don't know the whole story because Robert and I don't speak very often, but it seems a man showed up at the house one day and told Robert he would pay fair market value for the whole thing . . . the main house, guesthouse, stables, grounds, the lake . . . all of it. You must know Robert never particularly liked the house anyway. He always wanted to live in the city. So he took the offer. Apparently, he wasn't too keen on selling to this guy, but I think wanting out of the expense and obligation of keeping up the grounds got the better of him."

"Wow . . ." Angela trails off. Blythewood has been in the family for generations. She can't imagine someone other than a Wilcox living there.

Jon sees Angela's look of concern. "Are you okay? I know Blythewood meant so much to you."

"It's not my house to sell. It was a wonderful chapter of my life, living there, raising you . . ." She fluffs his thick wavy hair with her hand. "I'm sure Robert got a good price. And perhaps his disposition will improve if he's not tied to that estate."

"Yeow, Ange! ZING!"

They both pause and look at each other again. Angela is a tiny bit embarrassed and Jon is amazed at her candor. And then again they both burst out laughing.

"I LIKE this new Angela! Just what did Jack do to you?"

"I think I finally figured out some things about life."

"He seemed to have a real enjoyment for life."

"Yes . . . sometimes he just didn't seem real."

"He was real enough when I met him. And I could see he was crazy about you."

Angela helps Jon clean up the dishes and the kitchen. They sit a while in his living room, talking about his future plans and upcoming photography projects. And, again, he asks her to come live with him since he has plenty of room, and no fiancée to get in the way now.

"Oh—but I'm making my way now. I think I'm in a good place for the time being. I'm really feeling good about things." And hearing herself say the words, she finds she believes them.

CHAPTER 19

A few weeks later, Angela wakes to the sounds of banging on the roof and unfamiliar voices in the backyard. She jumps out of bed, pulls on her robe, and looks out her window. The back and front yards swarm with workers in various types of uniforms. Several crews are bustling around Beauregard; painters working on the lower levels of the house, restoring the robin's-egg blue and crisp white trim, and roofers climbing up ladders set against the house to replace the crumbling shingles. The porch boards and steps are being replaced and a sprinkler system installed to revive the yard and shrubs in high summer. The tree stump in the front yard is being ground and removed and a new willow tree waits to replace it, sitting on the lawn still in its burlap bag, bright green leaves waving in the breeze. A group of people are laying a new patio in the backyard, and even the broken-down shed at the far end of the yard is getting new boards and a coat of paint. It's as if the entire house is getting a face-lift. Angela dresses in a hurry and dashes downstairs.

She stops at the front desk in time to hear a man in coveralls with a telecommunications logo on the front of his uniform say to Bob, "Sir—the cable is all installed and I'll get your wireless modem set up now."

"That'll be just fine, young man," says Bob, gesturing toward his office.

"Bob! What is going on?"

Bob turns to her. "We are entering the twenty-first century."

"Who are all these people working?"

"We have been given a gift, Angela. A great gift."

"Who gives gifts like this?"

"I think you know ..." He peers at her over his reading glasses, then retreats to his office. Angela watches him go, perplexed. She just can't believe what is happening. It just can't be.

She opens the front door and sees that the workmen who had replaced the boards on the front porch are now building a new set of steps. And then a landscaping truck pulls up to the curb. It stops exactly where a cab had briefly parked that day ... The day she met Jack for the first time. A man in a pale green shirt and khaki pants jumps out of the truck, circles round to the back, and throws up the rolling door on the back of the truck. He starts pulling out rosebushes. Dozens and dozens of rosebushes. All of them yellow. If she'd had any doubt about who was responsible for this, the doubt has gone.

*   *   *

Once the work is complete, the whole mood of the house feels lighter and brighter. The tenants are thrilled with the improvements, and Wendy is in her element helping Bob understand how the new Internet connection and installation of wireless capability can improve their bookings. She hopes to talk him into a computer and online booking program to attract additional short-term guests.

Eventually, the tenants settle back into their respective routines once more, but with a renewed sense of the house. The backyard and patio are such pleasant places to linger now, as is the front porch with its fortified landing and steps. Henry has even bought himself a small tablet to read his paper, taking advantage of the in-house Internet. Wendy is thrilled to help him connect it, and is all the more excited that she can do her schoolwork on her laptop at the house, rather than squeeze it in between classes at school.

*   *   *

One morning as Angela opens the front door of the house to leave, a tall, thin, balding man with wire-rimmed glasses is standing on the other side, just about to knock. She thinks she has seen him before, but just can't remember where.

"Good morning! Is Jack Ford here?"

Really, Angela had thought she was over this. She clearly isn't doing as well as she thought she was if the mention of Jack's name by a stranger can cause her such pain, however slight. "No . . . no, he's not here."

"Oh. I came to give him season tickets to our symphony concerts. He gave us a very generous donation, and I thought I would deliver the tickets in person."

"Well, we don't have a forwarding address, so I'm not sure where to send them. A generous donation?"

"I should say so. He donated $50,000 at one of our concerts! We couldn't believe it! I say, are you all right?"

It must have been obvious that she had come close to fainting. She takes hold of herself. "Yes, yes . . . I just didn't realize he had made such a large donation." She composes herself, the old hurt creeping back into her heart—and demeanor. "I'm sorry—I can't tell you where to forward those tickets. Perhaps donate them to someone that could really enjoy them. I'm sure he would have approved."

"Perhaps you would care to have them? I seem to recall seeing you at a concert with him?"

"No . . . no thank you. Please find someone else to give them to."

"Thank you. I will." And the man bows slightly, turns and steps off the porch, and walks away down the street.

Angela is bewildered. She closes the door behind her and sits on the top step of the porch trying to make sense of what has been happening lately. All the work on the house, the painting, the roof, the roses . . . were those also "donations"? Jack had always seemed to have money and she suspected there was more to his work than he had ever let her know. Where did he get the resources to give such large gifts? Just who was he really? She supposes he will always be a mystery.

*   *   *

In the following days, Angela finds a new routine, a new rhythm. Rising early in the morning to open the coffee shop, she has some free time after closing the shop to wander or job hunt and be ready for dinner at the house. Since the house now has newly installed Internet, she has resumed job hunting using her laptop from the comfort of her own room. She also keeps up with news and local events, and has embraced email correspondence with Jon. It's all working out quite nicely.

She could never wish that Jack had not appeared in her life. Not only had he provided distraction and support, he'd also given her the resources to find another way to live her life and feel relevant. She's a changed person from the desperate, displaced, and destitute widow. She is now confident and self-sufficient. It may not be the life she dreamed of, but it's a good life.

CHAPTER 20

One afternoon, Angela is browsing the employment listings in the local paper and comes across a huge ad that sounds perfect for her.

Personal Assistant 'Angel'

Executive Personal Assistant needed for newly relocated president of multinational engineering firm. Must have actual and working knowledge of the corporate world and have extensive experience in the following duties:

Manage personal calendar, correspondence, and expenses

Plan and execute corporate events, charity fundraisers, and speaking engagements

Act as president's representative with visiting corporate partners

Manage personal household staff and day-to-day operations

Requirements include: basic computer skills, email, spreadsheets . . .

She doesn't need to read any further. This is it. It could have been written with her in mind. She writes a cover letter and attaches it and her résumé to an email. Of course, she knows how long it is likely to take before a reply comes, but still she can barely settle down that night. She's been looking for the position that was exactly right for her and this is it. A corporate position with duties she could do in her sleep. She can't help thinking what this position would do for her . . . she could get back out in the world, get her own place, be back on the social scene . . .

She thinks about Beauregard, the other tenants, the kindness of Bob and Wendy. Could she actually be sad to leave? After all these years of bemoaning her life here, would she now have regrets about moving on? Well, if she gets the job, she'll visit often. She'll bring surprises like Jack has. Not on that scale, obviously, but with the same amount of affection. She sighs, thinking of Jack again. She is grateful to him for teaching her the basic computer skills that have made her confident in applying for positions. She has come to be thankful for so many things about Jack. When she drifts off to sleep, her final thoughts are positive feelings about how well prepared she is for anything this position would require of her.

She wakes the next morning with a start. What time is it? She jumps out of bed and finds she's way ahead of her alarm. She knows what this is: she's a bundle of nervous energy hoping for an early response to her résumé submission. She needs to get her expectations under control—it could be weeks before she hears anything. She washes and dresses in a hurry and slips down the stairs and out the door.

The coffee shop is busy that morning, but everything goes smoothly enough. She feels particularly friendly, as if privy to a great secret no one else knows. After she closes up the shop, she is tempted to run back to the house and check for a response. She tells herself it will take longer than a day to respond, but she isn't really listening.

She gets back to the house just in time for dinner.

Wendy has noticed Angela's new confidence. "Miss Angela—you're just glowing! What's happened?"

"I'm pretty excited about something but I don't want to say anything until I have more information."

Wendy's face breaks into a wide smile. "OH—I'm so thrilled for you! I can't wait to hear all about it!"

Angela finishes her meal quickly and dashes up the stairs. She opens her laptop nervously. Two new emails! One is from Jon—but the other is from the email address in the job ad!

Dear Ms. Wilcox,

We were quite impressed with your credentials and would like you to visit our offices as soon as possible for an interview. Please let us know your earliest availability.

It takes all her self-control to keep Angela from dancing around the room. She doesn't want something as important as this interview to take place on a day when she has been working at the coffee shop, so she replies that she can be available at one day's notice. That way, she can arrange time off with Frank. She has never asked for any, and has been punctual since day one. She hates to leave him shorthanded, but it will be only for one day.

She has saved some money and she decides to visit the area's fine dress shop for a new suit to wear for interviews. Perhaps new shoes and bag, a pretty scarf. If the hair stylist has an opening, she'll pop in for a trim and deep conditioning to keep the frizz under control. Taking all that into account, she replies that the day after tomorrow would suit her.

The reply is immediate.

> *The day after tomorrow would be fine. Would 11:00 work for you?*

Oh my goodness! That was fast! She replies:

> *Yes – that would be perfect. I look forward to meeting you. Thank you.*

Next comes a message with the address and directions. It's really happening. After all this time, she can't believe it. All she'd had to do was let go of the desperation and the opportunity had come to her. Exactly as she had told herself it would. What else would show up if she just let go?

She sleeps well that night. Next day, after she's cleaned up and closed the shop, she asks Frank if she can take the next day off. He agrees. She thanks him and says she'll be back the morning after next.

*   *   *

The morning of her interview, she wakes early. She pulls the stunning amethyst-colored wool crepe suit out of its bag and lays it on her bed. She takes a long warm shower, taking special care of her hair and skin. She keeps her makeup light and pulls her shining hair into a loose chignon at the base of her neck which shows off the silver streaks in the most flattering way. Over her silk lingerie and stockings she slips on a pale purple silk blouse and conservative but elegant amethyst drop earrings. The suit goes on effortlessly without binding or bunching anywhere. She already has some timeless black leather pumps, with a matching clutch saved from her big clothing purge. She stands in front of the full-length mirror and sighs. This is it. It has to be.

She calls for a car so she'll be sure to arrive on time and unrumpled.

At the bottom of the stairs, she bumps into Wendy. "Oh my—you look amazing! Is this a special day?"

"I hope so. Wish me luck!" Angela calls as she dashes out the door.

*   *   *

The car pulls up to the address Angela had given the driver and she peers out the car window to look up at a monstrous skyscraper. "Are you sure this is the right place?"

"Yes, ma'am. I'm sure."

"Oh . . . well, thank you . . ." She pays the driver, steps onto the curb, and walks across the tree-enclosed pavement toward the building's entrance. The revolving doors reveal a grand lobby with shimmering silver walls and gleaming marble floors. She checks in at the enormous front desk and is ushered through the turnstile and onto the elevator by an attendant. The elevator interior is a mixture of the same gleaming silver chrome and dark wood insets. The carpet is spotless.

The elevator stops at the forty-fifth floor and she steps out into a large, marble-lined reception area facing a long, imposing, wood front desk staffed by two professionally dressed young women. On either side of the desk are sets of glass doors leading down white hallways lined by offices between which people are moving. It looks a hive of activity behind those glass doors.

Only now does she begin to feel nervous. This is all a little too much—and there's so much at stake. She feels as though she's walking into a dream. Taking a deep breath, she approaches the desk and gives her name to one of the women, saying she has an appointment.

"Certainly, Miss Wilcox. I'll let the president's administrator know you're here. If you'd like to take a seat, someone will be right along to collect you."

"Thank you." She turns and sees rather comfortable chairs in the reception area but she is too nervous to sit. She glances at a clock over the desk. 10:43. Good timing. Not too early; certainly not late. She turns when she hears one of the glass doors opens and the clack of heeled shoes walking across the marble floor toward her.

"Miss Wilcox. So nice to meet you. Please follow me." The woman smiles warmly as she motions toward the door through which she has just come.

"Thank you." Angela notes that the woman holds back a step to walk with her and not in front of her. Somehow she suddenly feels more comfortable. So far, all the staff have been professional and friendly.

Each side of the long hallway is lined with offices with glass walls that allow sunlight from the windowed offices to stream through to the other side and throughout the hallway. In most, people are working at large drafting tables. In one she notices several people gathered around a white board, discussing what looks on the board like technical ideas. In another, someone is printing blueprints on a huge plotter.

At the end of the hall they walk through another set of glass doors into what appears to be a spacious front office. On the desk is a phone console with a row of buttons, stacks of files and notebooks, a large laptop, and a desk lamp. Several file cabinets line one wall. There are chairs matching those in the lobby with a table between them. A stack of pictures leans against a far wall, waiting to be hung.

The woman leads her through this office and opens wide a set of dark, smoked glass doors. She steps through them. To Angela she says, "Please come in." She points toward a chair. Then she says, "Sir? Angela Wilcox is here for the interview."

As she walks into the huge sprawling office she is immediately struck by the bright sunlight streaming into the room through an entire wall of windows at the back of the office. The office is sparsely furnished. At one end of the room is a long folding table with papers, blueprints, and notebooks strewn about, and a couple of odd side chairs against the wall. Boxes are piled in corners. Standing in the center of the room, she faces an enormous dark wood executive desk with a large leather chair behind it. The back of the chair is to the door, preventing her from seeing who is sitting in it.

As the receptionist leaves, closing the door behind her, the large leather chair swings around. Angela just about falls over.

"Angela? A pleasure to meet you!" says that signature smile.

"Jack!" she gasps.

He is dressed in a fine custom-tailored suit, his hair slicked back, and clean shaven. He looks like a new man. "Well . . . aren't you a sight for sore eyes." He beams, that mischievous broad grin spreading across his face. "Excuse the mess . . . We've just moved in. I understand you're here about a position

I have available." He leans back in his chair and sets his elbows on the chair arms, touching his fingertips together in front of his chin.

"I don't understand . . . ?" She collapses into a chair in front of the desk. She had for a moment thought she might actually faint.

"I opened a branch office of my company here so I could be close to my daughter. And my grandchild."

"Your . . . daughter . . ." It finally all makes sense. "Jack, I'm afraid I've made a terrible mistake!"

"Don't worry about it. Kara told me the whole story. After she calmed down." He chuckles. "She was very angry with you. But that was on my behalf, and the only person I was angry with was me for not telling you earlier what was going on. She's come round now. I think you and she could be very good friends."

"Oh, Jack—I've been a prize idiot."

"No you're not. That sort of thinking gets no one anywhere. It's the future we have to think about, not the past. I bought a house, by the way. Quite a grand house. I think you're familiar? They call it Blythewood."

Angela's eyes grow wide. No wonder Robert was so strange about selling the house. He sold it to a Wilcox Corporation competitor.

"So—I need someone to help me get settled and take care of personal business for me. I understand you're a can-do sort of person."

"I think I am," she stutters.

"I need you to manage my personal calendar."

"I can do that."

"I need you to plan and execute company social events and fundraisers."

"I can do that."

"I need you to hire and oversee my household staff."

"I can do that."

"I need you to . . . be my partner . . . for life?"

Her breath catches in her throat. ". . . I can do that," she whispers.

Forty years melt from Jack's frame. He jumps from his chair and practically leaps over the desk to sweep her up in his arms. He embraces her, whispering in her ear, "My angel, my angel."

She wraps her arms around him and vows to herself never to let go again.

CHAPTER 21

It is a beautiful, perfect spring morning. The sun is shining and the slight breeze carries the scents from a variety of early blooming spring flowers and bushes. Beauregard is in its glory. Resplendent in its clean, vibrant robin's-egg blue with crisp white trim, it is the most magnificent home on the street, a testament to the architecture of its era. The young willow tree in the front yard is firmly established and growing rapidly. It will soon welcome future visitors to relax and enjoy its shade. The lawn is green and lush, and the yellow rosebushes and revitalized laurel and rhododendron bushes are full of buds, ready to burst. It will be spectacular this spring.

More than a boardinghouse, Beauregard is now a welcoming full-fledged guesthouse, with permanent guests, and an increasing number of travelers coming to stay for a night or two, taking advantage of the free Wi-Fi and excellent cuisine.

Behind the front desk, Bob and Wendy have their heads together over the computer Wendy has installed. She is reviewing with him the upcoming reservations on their computerized booking system. She also shows him how she can update and print menu cards as they expand their offerings. While Bob is somewhat suspicious of technology, he is truly engaged and hanging on her every word, beaming and proud of the young woman she has become.

She is wearing a familiar crisp navy linen blazer, the very one Angela wore on a hot, humid summer day some time ago.

She and Bob agree on a layout for the menu cards, and she will coordinate with Cook what the evening meal will offer. As she steps out from behind the front desk, a flurry of her brightly colored full-length tiered skirt follows her, skimming over a pair of red Mary Janes.

*   *   *

The dogwood trees are in bloom at Blythewood, the lilacs are bursting with their intoxicating scent, and a small patch of lily-of-the-valley flowers has sprung up at the end of the cook's garden, adding their sweet scent to the clear morning air. All the gardens are waking up under the watchful eye of an attentive gardening staff, continually clearing, and pruning, fertilizing, and weeding.

Always the early riser, Jack sits at the table on the back patio reading a newspaper. A silver coffee-and-tea service is on the table, along with a variety of baked breakfast items. He looks up and smiles broadly when he sees a glowing Angela step out the back door to join him for breakfast. She comes up behind him, placing her hands on his shoulders, and leans over to kiss him tenderly on the cheek. He reaches up to take one of her hands in his to kiss it. She moves around to the other side of the table to pour herself tea, and slides into a chair across from him. She looks out over the grounds of her precious Blythewood and toward the lake that shimmers in the spring sun. She turns back to him and notices him watching her. She blushes. She had never expected to be this happy again.

The back door opens again and Kara walks onto that patio with a toddler in tow. She walks over and embraces Jack and then Angela, as Jack sweeps the giggling little girl up in his arms and hoists her high above his head while she squeals with delight. She is the spitting image of her mother and Jack could not be a more doting grandfather.

Kara sits next to Angela and the women put their heads together, chatting and giggling together as Jack puts the baby in her high chair, tickling her toes and offering tiny bites of a buttery croissant. They look up to see Jon who has walked around the side of the house to the back patio to come join them. Angela waves him over to the table to sit with them. He embraces Angela warmly and vigorously shakes Jack's hand as he pats him on the opposite shoulder. Jack gestures to Kara in an introduction to Jon, who are both obviously happy to see each other . . . sparks fly?

Jack sits down and leans back in his chair as he looks over his new family, new life, new loves. He smiles widely and thinks . . . Ain't life grand.

ABOUT THE AUTHOR

Raised in sleepy northeast Connecticut, Allison Smith lived many years in New York before migrating to Colorado where she currently resides with her rescue cats, Alexandra and Duchess. She's been a professional pianist, business executive, commercial property manager, and marketing consultant.

Allison has always been writing, either professionally or for pleasure. She dabbled in pet poems and illustrated children's stories before focusing on fiction. *The New Tenant* is her first book.